# SIX SHORTS:

## A Devotional Study of Literary Devices in the Bible

Alisa Hope Wagner

Marked Writers Publishing

**SIX SHORTS: A Devotional Study of Literary Devices in the Bible**



Marked Writers Publishing
www.alisahopewagner.com

---

Scriptures taken from various translations of the Bible found at www.biblegateway.com.

---

Cover illustrations by Albert Morales
Author Photo by Lori Stead at https://www.wetsilver.com/

---

ISBN: 978-1-963190-06-9

# SIX SHORTS:

## A Devotional Study of Literary Devices in the Bible

Alisa Hope Wagner

# Dedication

Daniel – the man of my dreams

Isaac Jeremiah – my prophet

Levi Daniel – my shepherd

Karis Ruth – my graceful companion

Editing Team – Emerald Barnes, Patricia Coughlin, Cynthia Faulkner, Faith Newton, Holly Smith and Daniel Wagner

Illustrator – Albert Morales

Holy Spirit – my Writing Partner

# Acknowledgments

This book has been years in the making. I write my short stories sporadically when an idea hits me. I've written others that are found in some of my non-fiction books to emphasize the spiritual theme I'm discussing. However, these six I have been gathering for the right moment to publish. I knew God had a special plan for them, and I feel the value of what He wants to communicate to His people whom He loves so much.

I want to express my gratitude to my husband who supports my writing fiercely. Without him, I could not be the writer I am today. Also, I love that my kids—Isaac, Levi and Kiki—motivate me because I want to make them proud of me as I am proud of them.

Next, I want to give a huge thank you to my illustrator, Albert Morales, who breathes life into my stories with his spectacular illustrations.

Also, I am grateful to my editing team: Emerald Barnes, Patricia Coughlin, Faith Newton, Holly Smith and Daniel Wagner. Thank you for finding those pesky typos and for offering me encouragement and advice.

Finally, I want to thank my writing partner, the Holy Spirit. You are always by my side while I write, helping me wrestle with words. I couldn't have the victory without You

# TABLE OF CONTENTS

# INTRODUCTION

> "Most of us muddle along in predictable patterns. What imagination helps us see is that any life, no matter how ordinary, is extraordinary with God. He shattered ordinariness with the Incarnation. We just haven't gotten the message yet." – Cheryl Forbes, *Imagination: Embracing a Theology of Wonder*

We were created in God's image as free-thinking individuals endowed with the miracle of the imagination (Genesis 1:27). The imagination was gifted to us in the Garden of Eden. Let's imagine for a moment that the Garden of Eden is an actual place, but it is also symbolic of another place. **Symbolism** is a literary device that gives characters, objects, actions, places or other elements another, more profound meaning, or it can represent an abstract concept (aka a spiritual truth). The Garden of Eden symbolized the Presence of God or Heaven. Adam and Eve not only lived in the Garden of Eden, but they also dwelled within the Heavenly Presence of God. Garden of Eden = God's Presence.

God planted two trees in the Garden of Eden—along with everything else Adam and Eve would need to live peaceful, satisfying and perfect lives (Genesis 2:9). One of the trees was the Tree of Knowledge of Good and Evil. This tree is an actual tree, but it also has a greater symbolic meaning. It represents our ability to have free will, and imagination would be impossible without it. God gives us the ability to choose to obey or disobey because He wants imaginative children not unthinking robots.

We have the free will to use our imagination for good or evil. However, this gift of free will comes at a price. We can taste it and experience evil and feel shame. Before Adam and Eve disobeyed God and ate from the Tree of Knowledge, they felt no shame (Genesis 2:17 & Genesis 2:25). They allowed the words of the serpent (symbolic of Satan) to cause their imaginations to wonder about the tree and then acted on their inclinations (Genesis 3:1-7). Therefore, humankind fell from God's best, and we lost our perfect position with Him because He can have nothing to do with sin (Romans 3:23 & James 1:13). Adam and Eve had to leave God's Presence, but God had a plan to bring His Presence back to His children through the death and resurrection of Jesus, the Messiah.

God is love (1 John 4:16). He created us, so we could enjoy His love. He gives us the choice to love Him back, and true love is found in both words and deeds, not simply in feelings (though feeling loved by God is wonderful). We love God by trying our best to use our imaginative free will to create beauty for His glory. But since God knew we would fall short of His holy standard, He also put another tree in the Garden: The Tree of Life (Romans 3:23, Genesis 2:9 & Genesis 3:22, 24). This tree also had a profound symbolic meaning as well. It represents Jesus Christ, the Resurrection and the Life, Who washes away all our sin (John 11:25 & Hebrews 10:10). Jesus's Finished Work on the Cross cleanses our acts of free will that are done outside of God's will and perfects all our acts of free will that are done inside of God's will (1 John 1:7 & Titus 2:14).

This is why God rested on the seventh day (Genesis 2:2). Jesus said He is Lord over the Sabbath because that is when He did His work on the Cross—while God rested, redeeming all good six days that God created but that we corrupted with our free will to sin (Mark 2:27-28). The Sabbath (a day of rest) was created as an actual day, but the literary device of **symbolism** gives this day a greater meaning. Jesus promised us He would give us the Holy Spirit after His death and resurrection (John 14:26). Therefore, we are now living in a time of Sabbath, not simply a day. We exist in an era where we can rest from our constant striving to be perfect. Jesus swapped our sin for His righteousness, and now we have Heaven (God's Presence) within us! The gift of free will mandated two trees to satisfy God's desire for perfection and love. The Tree of Knowledge gives us free will to choose. The Tree of Life redeems and perfects our free will choices.

The Bible is brimming with literary devices. **Symbolism** is just one example. The Holy Spirit opens the living aspect of the Bible to us, making it no longer just a book of historical stories (Hebrews 4:12). He guides us as we read the Bible, giving us insights and applying spiritual truths to our current situation. But how much more understanding would we gain if we could recognize literary devices? Literary devices are used to enhance writing, creating a more profound impact on the readers. Today, we are bombarded with images. We don't need literary devices to form those images in our mind and produce those feelings in our heart. We have decorations in our homes. We watch television and movies. We can see all kinds of landscapes around the world. And the world is filled with endless photos, memes and reels on social media.

Our acquaintance with literary devices is diminishing, and it is affecting our Bible reading, producing confusion and ignorance and causing division in the Church. The writers of the Bible used literary devices because their main form of entertainment and sharing information was by using their words with no visual aids. Their words alone had to convey spiritual awareness to readers and listeners by producing images, emotions and understanding. Thus, literary devices were imperative in ancient times when the Bible was written.

My heart in writing this book is to use my education and experience to help us gain a better understanding of literary devices, so that when we read the Bible, we can look deeper into what the Holy Spirit was communicating through Biblical writers, and what He is communicating to us currently. The Bible is abounding with God's promises that are potentially ours. I say potentially because we can't claim what we don't know. I want our Bible reading time to fill our minds, hearts, bodies and wills with God's love, truth, victory, freedom, joy, healing and every good thing found in the pages of His Word.

Each of my six short stories will have a devotional study and reflection questions based on the story and five literary devices pulled from the short story along with the corresponding literary devices pulled from the Bible. Therefore, we will learn thirty devices in all. My genre of choice is speculative (fantasy, dystopian, science-fiction, supernatural, etc.), so we can expect speculative aspects throughout each story. All the stories save one is spiritual in nature. I wrote the flash fiction story (around one thousand words) from a writer's perspective. It is not necessarily about faith, but it does focus on a moral issue we all face but that we writers face specifically. I pray that my stories not only entertain us, but that they teach, move and grow us. I want us to be able to take what we learn and allow the literary devices found in the Bible to reveal themselves, offering us greater clarity, insight, wisdom and anticipation—thus, giving us more victory in our daily lives. I use the word "us" because I am learning along with you, yearning for the ears that will hear and discern the voice of God.

> *"Then Jesus said, 'Whoever has ears to hear, let them hear'" (Mark 4:9 NIV).*

# FICTION: A TOOL OF JESUS

Jesus penned forty-six parables. Parables are short fiction stories that help moral truths infiltrate the audience's minds and hearts. Although He didn't write them down personally, these parables left such an impact on His followers that they are included in all four Gospel accounts.

> ***par·a·ble***
> ***Noun***
> ***a simple story used to illustrate a moral or spiritual lesson***

Jesus knew that fiction would resonate with His listeners and, eventually, His readers. Like a magic portal, a story sweeps us into another life and world and allows us to imagine and feel circumstances outside of ourselves. We walk in another's shoes and see life from a different vantage point. And before we know it, a truth has been planted so deep within our spirits that we can't shake it. We have been entertained, informed and maybe even changed.

What makes a parable resonate is what makes all stories resonate. Jesus is the Word (John 1:1) and, thus, He is the Master Writer. He knew what would make His stories connect with His audience: ***Conflict creates tension that leads to change.***

With 21 verses, the *Parable of the Prodigal Son* is the longest of them all. Jesus was surrounded by an audience of tax collectors and Pharisees who all knew the Law well. The sinners knew they fell short, so they stopped trying, and the Pharisees manhandled the Law to fit their own deficiencies. But what of grace?

With all eyes on Him, Jesus does not offer a non-fiction bullet-list definition of grace. He tells them a story (Luke 15:11-32).

*There were two sons. The younger son was not satisfied living in his father's house.*

- **Conflict:** The son's viewpoint differs from his father's.
- **Tension:** There is a rift between father and son.
- **Solution:** The son demands his money and leaves home to indulge in wild living.

*The son quickly spends all of his inheritance as a famine spreads across the land.*

- **Conflict:** The son is broke.
- **Tension:** He must find work during an economically difficult time.
- **Solution:** He survives by feeding pigs, an animal that, to him, is culturally unclean.

*The son is still hungry and looks longingly at the pigs' food.*

- **Conflict:** The son is starving to death.
- **Tension:** He realizes he cannot survive on his own.
- **Solution:** He decides to humble himself and return home.

*The son goes back home to beg his father for a servant's position in the estate.*

- **Conflict:** The son must face his father.
- **Tension:** The rift between father and son still exists.
- **Solution:** Surprise ending, GRACE.

The father loves his son so much that when he spies him yet in the distance, he picks up his robes, and like a child, runs passionately to him. He grabs hold of his youngest son, hugging and kissing him, and does not say a word of the money and time that he squandered. The father does not give him a position of a servant; rather, he sets him up as co-heir of the estate with his signet ring.

- **Climax:** *The father throws a party because his son who was once lost has made his way home.*

But wait. Jesus' audience doesn't quite understand the story. The son did not get what he deserved. The Law was not met. A party has replaced punishment, and celebration has replaced recompense.

Like the audience, the older son doesn't understand this thing called grace. He is angry and won't join in the fun. Why should his brother who deserves to be reprimanded be acquitted so easily? Where is justice? Where is punishment? The older son has labored under the Law like a slave. He doesn't need grace nor does he want it. He is perfect in his own eyes.

I'm sure the Pharisees listening to Jesus' story began to pace with agitation, as the sinners in the crowd dared to grasp onto hope. The Law was too hard. They could never be good enough. Could there be another way to the Father's house besides perfection? This thing called *grace* seemed too good to be true, but as Jesus ended His Parable, the truth of grace fitted itself deep within the heart of every listener to be either rejected or received.

> *"But God demonstrates his own love for us in this: While we were still sinners, Christ died for us" (Romans 5:8 NIV).*

Grace is a gift for all who see their need for it. The younger son saw his deficiencies and became a true son. The older son saw his righteousness and became a slave. Humility releases freedom; pride holds enslavement. Grace goes to those who realize they are sinners. That is the moral of Jesus' parable, and this fiction piece is at the heart of the entirety of God's Word. Like the young son, we have each gone astray. We all need a Savior.

> *"But he was pierced for our transgressions, he was crushed for our iniquities; the punishment that brought us peace was on him, and by his wounds we are healed. We all, like sheep, have gone astray, each of us has turned to our own way; and the LORD has laid on him the iniquity of us all" (Isaiah 53:5-6 NIV).*

How could Jesus possibly explain this thing called grace to the crowd without parables? Jesus ignited the imagination of all His listeners, painting the expression and realization of grace across every soul with His stories. Needless to say, grace could not be explained without fiction rooted in truth. Christian fiction changed history through the parables of Jesus.

And that's what we as Christian fiction writers have been gifted and honored to create: fiction rooted in truth. Our hearts are anchored in God's as we spin tales that offer our readers a glimpse of imperfect lives embraced by grace. No matter our genre, there is no greater story than when our protagonists cannot overcome the final obstacle on their own. The surprise ending happens when there is outside intervention that offers the solution.

How bold and awesome is a main character who sets out on a journey knowing it cannot be accomplished? Frodo from the *Lord of the Rings Trilogy*, determined for Mordor, knew the odds were against him and that the chance of victory was slim, but he had a high calling (to save the world) and he stepped out by faith. At the edge of the fire, he had to face his own pride. An outside force of mercy bit off his finger (Gollum), and his brokenness became his solution. The ring was finally overcome, and once again grace is lodged in the hearts of the readers.

- **Conflict:** We are separated from our Creator because of sin.
- **Tension:** We can't have a relationship with our Heavenly Father.
- **Solution:** Jesus died on the Cross, vanquishing sin, so we could have a relationship with Him.

The Covenant of Salvation is the hope for all of us. We are drawn to the underdog story because we see ourselves in it. We cannot overcome in this life alone. We must have divine intervention. When we read Jesus' parables, we get a sense of God's divine purpose. He knew we would fall short (Romans 3:23). God knew we couldn't overcome on our own (Ephesians 2:8-9), which is why He had the solution—grace through the Finished Work of Jesus on the Cross.

Grace cannot simply be explained. It must be shown in a parable, in a story, in a life. Therein lies the truth of fiction: it has the power to not only entertain and inform but to change the world. It is a tool victory, cutting away indifference and ignorance. Jesus used this tool at least forty-six times during His ministry. He knew that some of the most important universal truths could only be discovered in fiction. And as we will discover, He used literary devices to help engage His audience even more.

# THE HAT SHOPPE

Devon jumped from the final step of the city bus, not caring what the other passengers thought about his childish gesture. He'd waited for this day most of his life. He had achieved something his family had never accomplished. He graduated from college. He took his last test an hour ago, and the professor graded it on the spot. He passed and earned his business degree. In a few days, he would walk the stage and take hold of his best life, but first he had a promise to keep.

He looked around at the tall buildings of the city. He would visit the city as a kid and walk down important sidewalks as bustling buildings jeered at him. Now sidewalks would bow, and buildings would stand at attention. His mother worked in the city all his life, cleaning rooms of elegant hotels with their ballrooms and swimming pools. She brought him to work on federal holidays when the schools were closed. Hotels never closed. Suits still worked, vacationers still played and his mother still cleaned.

That was the day he made the promise. He was eight years old on a Monday when he and his mom stepped off the city bus. The hotel she cleaned stared at him impatiently, not wanting to be bothered by a poor housekeeper's son.

It was after he'd seen the man that he made the promise to himself. The man awaited his driver outside the revolving golden doors of the hotel.

Young Devon hadn't noticed him at first until his mom stopped, knelt and pointed him out. The man wore a sleek grey suit with leather shoes and a felt hat. He looked like he belonged in the city, and Devon felt out of place in his jeans, t-shirt and worn-out tennis shoes.

"You see that man?" his mom asked.

"Yes, Mama," he answered, noticing that the hotel seemed to lean away from the man in awe.

"He's a businessman. You can be like him someday, but you must get your college degree. Do you understand?"

The boy quickly moved his gaze from the businessman to his mother's serious stare. He felt the weight of her words, and they dropped into his soul like handfuls of acorn seeds that scattered the dusty ground of his school's playground. He nodded solemnly and stared back at the man in the suit. He was stepping into a shiny SUV. "I like his hat, Mama. When I become a businessman, can I get a hat like his?"

His mother gently nudged her calloused finger into the backpack he held. "You can get any hat you want. Plus, you can stay in fancy hotels and ride in their shiny SUVs. And I will be so proud of you."

"Yes ... but, Mama," he whispered, "where do I get a hat like that?"

His mom smiled and leaned back on the thick soles of her cheap, orthopedic shoes. "I overheard him asking the concierge where he could purchase a nice felt hat. They sent him to the hat shop only a few blocks from the hotel. It has been there for almost a hundred years, and it has many hats to choose from. The hats from that shop are very well made, yet very expensive. I'll take you there after work, and you can look into the window. Would you like that?"

The boy nodded his head fervently.

"Okay," his mom said, standing. "Now we must go. I can't punch in late."

Tension stole Devon's childhood memory, as the shadow of the hotel fell across the section of the city where the bus let him out. He could have gotten off at the next stop and been closer to the hat shop, but he needed the hotel to take note. Devon leveled his chin and puffed out his chest while swinging his arms and legs in long, purposeful strides. The next time that hotel saw him, he would have a college degree of prestige in his hand. He would no longer be strapped to a ratty, old backpack of humiliation.

As Devon reached the windows of the hat shop, he hesitated. He had never walked into the window-framed image of fashionably flaunted hats before. The scene seemed to him more of a painted illusion, but it would momentarily become a firsthand reality. A sun-faded sign that read, "Selling

Hats for 100 Years," winked at him from one of the glass-paned sections of the door. He promptly fumbled for the bills in the right pocket of his slacks. He worked on campus to supplement the scholarships and grants he had received. Each month, he'd collect every crumb of coinage that clattered onto his table. Finally, he exchanged the scraps of cash for five fresh Benjamins rolled up like brass knuckles in his pocket ready to break the ceiling of lack over his life.

He could have waited until his first paycheck to secure his hat. The college career services helped him receive a paid internship with a bank thanks to his minor in finance, but paychecks were for practical things, like rent and food. This purchase, however, was a declaration to the universe that his will would rewrite the unfolding scroll of time. He would buy the businessman's felt hat and walk the sidewalks that once shooed him away. Then, busy buildings would open their arms to him, but only a hat from this shop would do. His mom had said so, and she stressed that they were expensive. Determinedly, Devon grabbed the curved brass door handle of the shop and stepped inside.

Devon's skin soaked up the smells of the hat shop, absorbing the aromas of wealth and affluence. If ever he designed his own cologne, it would smell like this moment, and he would douse his suit daily in its self-assured essence. An elderly man appeared next to him, and his smile stretched across his aged cheeks into his wrinkled eyes. "My name is Eleazar, but my customers and friends call me Ellie. I am the owner of this hat shop. It has been in my family for over a century. I can see that you are a young man in need of a good hat, and I am ready to assist you in that endeavor. Our hats are each handmade with the finest natural materials. You will not find better workmanship with more integrity on this side of the continent."

The intimidation Devon had unknowingly carried into the hat shop dissolved, and he withdrew his right hand from his pocket of money and offered his hand to Mr. Ellie, the hat shop owner. He had never questioned the cost of the hats. His mom had said that they were the best, and he took her convictions by faith. However, the shop owner's statement of quality added a measure of assurance to his acquisition. "Good afternoon, Mr. Ellie. My name is Devon DeWitt, and I just earned my college degree. I'm here to purchase a felt hat, so I can begin my career in the city."

The old shop owner took Devon's hand into his calloused palm and gave it a few good shakes. Something about his fingers reminded Devon of his mother, and he knew more than ever that he was meant to be there. The rest of his life began here, and suddenly, the weight of his momentary choice fell on him like four years of learning squeezed into a single, dense second. The rows of arranged hats called out to him, and the five one-hundred-dollar bills in his pocket burned. Perspiration gathered on his forehead, and an image of staining his new felt hat with sweat stabbed his chest with fear.

The old shop owner seemed to notice the change in Devon's countenance, and he nodded with understanding. He placed his calloused hand on Devon's shoulder and peered into his anxious expression. "Don't you worry one bit," the old owner affirmed. "I'll help you find the right fit and hat. I've been helping my customers for a very long time. There are indeed many hats to choose from and lots of styles and colors to consider, but we can whittle down the choices a great deal once I get your size and you tell me what you are looking for."

An air of relief filled Devon's lungs, and his heavy chest lifted lightly. "Mr. Ellie, I'm looking for a felt hat, and when I see it, I will know."

The old shop owner gave a meaningful nod. "I believe you will. Here," he said, as a measuring tape unfurled from his fingers. "Let me measure you for the perfect fit."

Devon leaned his head forward. He hadn't noticed the measuring tape in the shop owner's hand, but he was an expert hat maker and knew what he was doing. Devon felt Mr. Ellie place the tape's end above his left ear and wrap the length of it around the circumference of his head just across his eyebrows. Then he released the loose end and pinched the tape at the right measurement.

"Yep, just what I thought, but I wanted to be sure. Now follow me," Mr. Ellie said. The shop owner made his way into the middle of the showroom and waited for Devon to join him. Then he pointed to the far left. "Those are flat caps," he said. Then his pointed hand veered to the right, inch by inch, as he listed the rest of the hats. "Those are bucket hats. And those are bakerboy caps. Next are trilby hats and then Panama hats. And finally," he said, motioning to the far right, "those are fedoras. There are different designs within each collection, but you can at least make your way to the section of the store you favor most. Within each collection, we have different materials—felt, leather, tweed, linen, straw, silk, and more—but since you want felt, your choice will be even easier to make."

Devon realized there was more to the word *hat* than he had considered, but once he saw the shelves of fedoras, he knew where he needed to look. "Definitely the fedoras," Devon said confidently.

"I thought as much. Fedoras have a feel for the city. Why don't you make your way over there and examine each felt fedora closely? They may look similar from a distance, but I assure you they each have a distinctive design and hue. There are no wrong choices. Now that we know your size and desired collection, the rest is a matter of opinion and taste."

Devon waivered. He had all but forgotten about price. "I must also mention, although I have saved for many years, I do have a budget of no more than five hundred dollars."

"I respect your budget," Mr. Ellie assured. "Some folks come in here ill-prepared to hear the price. They either get angry and storm out of my shop or they become embarrassed and apologize. However, your budget should cover almost any felt hat in the store, save the top hats on the racks behind the register. I didn't mention those because they didn't fit your need."

Devon gave a low laugh of relief. "No, I will not be looking at top hats for a while. If you don't mind, I will look at your selection."

"Take your time," Mr. Ellie said. "I'll be checking my inventory list behind the register. Let me know if you need anything."

Devon watched the old hat shop owner step behind the counter of his register. He eyed the top hats lining the wall behind him. No, he didn't need one of those. He turned his gaze to the rows of elegant fedoras and made his way to their location.

Mr. Ellie was correct. There were many felt fedoras to choose from, and he could envision the businessman wearing each one. He reached his hand toward the taupe-colored fedora with a pinched shaped crown and narrow brim, but he stopped abruptly when a hissing voice came from behind.

"Are you sure that is the perfect one?" the tall man sneered. He wore a cream fedora that reflected the ceiling lights of the showroom. It had an exaggerated pinched crown, forming the two points of the letter "M" and an extra wide brim that shaded the man's face entirely.

"Mr. Ellie and I decided that I should choose my hat from here. I want a felt fedora, and this is my selection."

The man scoffed. "Why felt? What a boring material. My silk fedora glows."

"I am a young man. I want a hat that will last me," Devon said, trying to dismiss the man.

"Why would the owner even limit you here when there are hundreds of choices," the tall man pressed, spreading his arms like he owned the shop. "You cannot make this decision lightly. The price is too hefty for just any old hat."

Devon stepped back. He had been working toward this decision for years, and he didn't want to choose incorrectly. He did find the man's hat attractive. He looked to his left, and the other appealing collection of hats beckoned him—every color, every size, every design and every function bombarded his thoughts with what-ifs. He turned back to the man to seek further advice, but he was stunned to see that the man's silk, cream fedora was now replaced with a checkered, tweed flat cap that flopped across his face like a mourning veil.

"Did you change hats?" Devon asked in disbelief.

"Well, of course I did!" the man jeered. "Why would I want to be stuck with the same hat day after day, week after week and year after year when there are so many hats to choose from?"

Devon did find the man's hat intriguing. Then another hat captured Devon's side-gaze. It was one of the trilby hats. It was the same taupe color as the fedora he had picked out, but this one had a leather band around the bottom of the crown. "I do like that one also," he said, pointing. "It looks a lot like the fedora except the crown is not so pinched." He closed his eyes, remembering the businessman from when he was young. His hat had been a fedora, but he didn't have to match it exactly. The trilby would be nice.

Devon turned back to the tall man to get his opinion, but now he wore an oversized, linen bucket hat that hung over his ears and eyes like a stemless, grey mushroom. "You changed your hat again!"

A sly smile curled along the man's lips like a greasy mustache. "I don't keep the same hat for long. It bores me, so I must have something new."

Devon glanced back at the fedoras in front of him. The leather ones looked nice; although, they probably cost a lot more than the felt fedoras. He could see if Mr. Ellie would allow him time to pay the rest with his first paycheck. "What about leather?" Devon asked the tall man.

When he turned back, he was unable to suppress his shock as the man now wore a towering crimson top hat. "You changed it again!"

"Yes, and you can too. You shouldn't have to stick with just one hat. You can have any hat you choose. I have loads of credit at this store. Just put them in my name, and you can pay me back over time."

Devon's chest clinched as images of hats scattered his mind like cards flying out of a bad shuffle. He looked toward the cash register to find Mr. Ellie, but the shop owner was nowhere in sight. Suddenly, he no longer trusted the tall man's advice. He felt anxious and confused, like he was drowning under an endless pile of would-be hats. "No," Devon declared, directing his thoughts. "I will pick from the selection that Mr. Ellie and I already agreed upon." He looked back at the taupe-felt fedora he had examined first. He did like it, but it was a little bland.

"Would you like me to put a band around it?" the old shopkeeper asked.

Devon looked around. The tall man was gone, and Mr. Ellie stood at his side.

"Yes, I would like that. Will it be leather?" Devon asked.

"The leather band would go over your budget, but I have a fabric band that would look just as nice," Mr. Ellie said.

Devon took hold of his new hat. "Yes, that will be perfect."

"I'll box it up for you," the old owner said, taking the hat from Devon's hands.

"I'll take the box but don't pack up the hat. I want to wear it out," Devon said.

"I think that is a fine idea," the shop owner agreed. "You have chosen well."

When Devon exited the shop, a sunray reflecting off a city window shined on him like a spotlight. The sidewalk became his stage and the buildings his audience. He tilted the fedora with a gesture of greeting.

"Welcome to the city, Devon DeWitt!" the traffic roared. "To Devon Dewitt, the city offers its greeting!"

## Devotional Study

I got inspiration for this short story when we visited a hat shop on vacation. The shop was closing after a hundred years of being open. They had a sign posted on their door with the unhappy information. I was saddened by the look of the store as I gazed through the window. Boxes scattered the floor, and very few hats remained. They must have had a closing sale. I wish I could have bought a hat, but instead I wrote this short story to commemorate how the closing store made me feel. I didn't know much about hats, so I did a lot of research to prepare.

The hats represent our choices. The store owner represents God. The hissing customer represents Satan. And Devon DeWitt represents a young generation blasted by choices. The devil would like nothing more than to distract them from God's will with a plethora of choices, which causes confusion and will prevent them from fulfilling their destiny.

In our world today, we have so many choices that they can produce depression and anxiety. Did we marry the right person? Did we buy the right house? Did we choose the right career? Did we choose the right church? Did we move to the right city? Thankfully, God has a plan for our lives. However, I don't believe this plan has every detail strictly laid out. If we are headed in the right direction, God gives us creative license to paint our path with the colors of our choosing. There is freedom in knowing our purpose and not getting lost in all the possibilities. That's what Devon DeWitt learned. He finally listened to the direction of the shop owner and made his choice without all the other distractions of the world.

> "For I know the plans I have for you,' declares the LORD, 'plans to prosper you and not to harm you, plans to give you hope and a future'" (Jeremiah 29:11 NIV).

## Reflection Questions

Have you ever been bombarded by too many choices when an important decision needed to be made? How did having so many possibilities make you feel? How did you finally come to a conclusion? Did you seek the Lord when making your final choice? What was the result? Were you happy about the direction you went or not?

# 5 Literary Devices

1. **Antithesis:** Two sentences of contrasting meanings in close proximity to each other.

**Short Story:** "The next time that hotel saw him, he would have a college degree of prestige in his hand. He would no longer be strapped to a ratty, old backpack of humiliation."

**Bible:** *"Which of you, if your son asks for bread, will give him a stone? Or if he asks for a fish, will give him a snake?"* (Matthew 7:9-10 NIV).

2. **Chiasmus:** A two-part sentence or phrase with the two parts of the phrase mirroring each other. The elements of the first phrase will be flipped in the second.

**Short Story:** "Welcome to the city, Devon DeWitt!" the traffic roared. "To Devon DeWitt, the city offers its greeting!"

**Bible:** *"But many who are first will be last, and many who are last will be first"* (Matthew 19:30 NIV).

3. **Diatribe:** Angry speech used to criticize strongly and aggressively at or about someone or something.

**Short Story:** "Why would the owner even limit you here when there are hundreds of choices," the tall man pressed, spreading his arms like he owned the shop. "You cannot make this decision lightly. The price is too hefty for just any old hat."

**Bible:** *"Now the serpent was more crafty than any of the wild animals the LORD God had made. He said to the woman, 'Did God really say, "You must not eat from any tree in the garden?" ...You will not certainly die,' the serpent said to the woman. 'For God knows that when you eat from it your eyes will be opened, and you will be like God, knowing good and evil'"* (Genesis 3:1 & 4-5 NIV).

4. **Personification:** Giving human attributes to inanimate objects.

**Short Story:** "The hotel she cleaned stared at him impatiently, not wanting to be bothered by a poor housekeeper's son."

**Bible:** *"The waters saw you, God, the waters saw you and writhed; the very depths were convulsed"* (Psalm 77:16 NIV).

5. **Simile:** A comparison between two unlike things using "like" or "as."

**Shorty Story:** "He felt the weight of her words, and they dropped into his soul like handfuls of acorn seeds that scattered the dusty ground of his school's playground."

**Bible:** *"I am sending you out like sheep among wolves. Therefore be as shrewd as snakes and as innocent as doves"* (Mathew 10:16 NIV).

# THE ONE TREE

# Prologue

Aryan listened to his parents' fading murmurs. They had finally receded into the thick darkness that separated him from them. His mother's blanketed sobs had slipped down the cracks of the floorboards into the cellar of his new room. The vibrations of their voices painted vapors of fading colors along the dusk of the ceiling. The emptiness of the cellar only magnified the echoes, like stray rays sneaking out from a cloud-covered sun.

Just this morning his parents declared his brother a man who needed his own space. His older brother, Derik, kept the warm hearth next to their parents, and Aryan made his way down the wood-chopped steps into the earth chamber of their home. No longer would he be able to smell the salt of Derik's skin next to him. They were now two brothers separated because of their age.

He had tried to leave the cellar earlier that night, wanting a cool drink of water from the basin. But the opening leading to the main floor had been barricaded. He cried out for Derik, frustrated that he couldn't see his brother's form through the wood panels of the door. His eyes could only capture a slight glimpse of his straw-colored hair or a quick glance of his blue eyes that matched the midday sky.

The warm fire of the main hearth afforded just enough light to see portions, but no comforting touch could be given from the other side.

Aryan left the locked door and crawled back to his fiber-stuffed mattress on the floor. He peered into the void above and envisioned the blue of his brother's eyes, displaying them like stars across the wood planks of the floor hovering over him. The underbelly wood surface was smooth and unscathed by the constant footsteps that scuffed the other side. Why had his brother's eyes been rimmed in red? Aryan didn't understand. Did all boys cry when they were to become men? His mother had wept in the folds of her bed. Time transformed her firstborn into a man, and she mourned her loss. But what of him, the second-born son?

Aryan knew that the tears shed that night could not counter the cries they beheld only two moons ago. His best friend, Ryun, had been touched by the Walking Disease. A peddler had sold him a kicking stone made of a spongy material from a coastal village. Playing with that stone had been Ryun's favorite pastime every afternoon until his neck grew a red lesion that wept yellow. The day Aryan noticed his friend's sore would be the last day he would ever see him again.

Ryun's family forced him to follow the path that led to the Walker's Settlement—a path that

Ryun and Aryan avoided all their lives. The Walkers moaned every few nights when one of their own embraced death. Their sad howls rang of joy—sadness for the life lost and joy for the pain ended. Aryan listened for the Walker's sorrowful harmony every night, wondering if Ryun had wandered into eternity. It was too early still. Ryun's eyes had no abrasions when his parents banished him. The loss of the Walker's sight was the first sign that death would shortly come. Ryun was lost to them. He could never return home.

Aryan's nostrils flared. The winds had brought the scent of fired-consumed flesh. Once a week the Walker's burned their dead, sparing the living from their disease-encrusted carcasses. They would then bury the ashes several feet underground and plant a single seed from the One Tree. The seeds rarely survived. The One Tree did not grow well in the dampness of Northland. The Southland contained the loose, dry soil needed for their sinewy roots. But the few that did thrive marked the land with the hope of every Walker—a hope of returning home.

Aryan tried to cover his face with the thinly woven fabric of his blanket. It did not impede the smell of scorching rot from entering his lungs. Previous nights when the fires sent smoke to his hearth, his brother would listen to him while he softly chattered his thoughts. The words he sprinkled from his lips became like a soft covering around him, allowing sleep to finally overtake him. But his brother was no longer by his side, forcing the perfume of the dead to now share his bed. Aryan became angry at time for stealing his brother. Had the moon and sun halted their course, Derik would not have grown up. And things could have stayed like they were.

## Phase I

Aryan followed behind his older brother. He had been so glad to leave the cellar, but after months of searching for his mother's pregnancy root, he was ready to go home.

"Derik, I don't understand why we must walk at night," Aryan said, pulling at the wrappings around his arms. "I cannot see the trees in front of me. Every night is cloudy and dark and then you find a deep cave for us to sleep during the day. I haven't seen the sun in ages."

"Stop pulling at your covering. You know what Father said," Derik whispered sternly in the night. "The sun is brighter in the Southland, and our skin is not accustomed to its harsh rays. We have to keep these coverings on, so our skin does not burn. If we get burned, we must go home. If we go home without the pregnancy root, the twins won't make it to full term."

Aryan looked toward his brother's figure walking in front of him. He could barely make out his silhouette in the shadows of the forest. Instead, he envisioned the blue of his brother's eyes glinting in the sunlight. "The sun does not shine at night, Brother."

"Yes, but it lingers. It's always lingering. Already, you have a burn on your neck. I see you scratch at it. You are being reckless. Keep your covering tight around your skin. Isn't this better than being in the cellar?"

Aryan dropped his head. "Yes, I hated sleeping there. I'm glad Mother sent us on this quest to save her twins. I just hope we find the cure in time. She was already midterm before we left."

"Don't worry, Little Brother. I know we will find it. I feel it in my soul. The root only grows under the shade of the large One Trees that have enjoyed the dryness of Southland for uncountable moons. We are getting close. The air has become arid, and the rains have lessened. The land has become flat, and the natural springs are growing scarce," he said, patting the side of his tunic. "But Father gave me a flagon of water, though, for our journey back. We must resist the urge to drink until it's time. He gave me specific orders to follow."

Aryan fixed a memory of the night they left in his mind. “I saw Father talking with you for many moments before we set out on our journey. He even embraced you. Why did he not give me instructions too? Why did I not receive a hug? You are not even three years older than me. I, too, carry this burden of finding Mother’s root,” Aryan said. He was not supposed to have seen their conversation. Although it was night, it was his first time out of the cellar in many moons. He longed to see his family and absorb its love once more. It would be like diving into a lake after weeks of working the fields. Yet as he searched for his mother, he couldn’t find her. She had gone to bed early, and her door was shut.

Derik did not answer Aryan’s questions right away. His footsteps slowed but continued southward. Finally, he whispered over his shoulder. “Father didn’t want to scare you, but he knew this quest would be difficult. He told me to take care of you and make sure to bring you home safely,” Derik finished. “He wants everything to go back to normal when we return home. Now, let’s quiet our voices, lest we arouse the senses of a nocturnal predator.”

# Phase 2

Aryan turned onto his back. The ground of the cave was cool, and it felt good against his skin. Sleep did not come easily. He wanted to scratch at his coverings, but he knew his brother would yell at him. Both his and Derik's coverings were filthy, but they couldn't wash them because there was no water for cleaning. He felt dirty and tired and longed for home. He thought of his mother. She disappeared the night they left. He knew it must have been difficult to send her two sons on a mission to save the two unborn babies within her. Maybe she couldn't bear to watch them leave.

"Derik, are you awake?" he whispered, knowing his brother would wake up even if he were asleep.

"I am now," Derik said rolling over.

Aryan stared at his brother but could barely make out his figure in the darkness of the cave. "I was thinking of Mother. Remember when she started crying every night? I thought she was crying for you because you had become a man and now had to be separated. But now I look back on it, do you think she may have cried because—you know—it was the first sign of her pregnancy?"

Aryan waited. His brother was thinking. Derik liked to consider his words before releasing them.

Aryan decided to press his point further. "Ryun told me that when his mother became pregnant with his younger sister, she was very emotional. She would cry if a bird fell from her nest. He asked his father about it, and he told him that women cry more when they are with child."

Again, Aryan waited for his brother to reply.

"You think about Mother a lot, don't you?" Derik finally asked.

"No, it's not that. Well—yes, I do think of her. I miss her. Did you know that she used to run her fingers through my hair when she thought I was sleeping? Every night I would rush to our bed and wait for her to come in. She'd sneak in while you were still finishing up your evening chores. I'd feel her stroke my head. Sometimes I would hear her whisper words, but they were always too quiet for me to hear."

"Those weren't whispers," Derik said softly. "They were prayers. Mother used to stroke my hair and pray over me too. I told her to stop, though, when I got too old."

"I never told her to stop," Aryan said, anger rising in his voice. "She probably stopped for both of us when you told her to. I'm younger than you. I still wanted those nights with her."

"I'm sorry, Brother. It was my fault. I shouldn't have said anything," Derik said.

Aryan noted that his brother's voice sounded sorrowful. "It's okay. I know you had become a man, which is why we could no longer share the same bed. And you are the oldest and work the hardest, so you deserved to stay in our hearth. The nights in the cellar were lonely. I only wish ..."

"What?"

"Father said he saw Ryun trying to get into our home. He was afraid that he would try to give me the Walking Disease, so I would be forced to go with him to the settlement," Aryan said.

"And that's why you had to stay in the cellar during the day. Mother was afraid that Ryun would get you sick and take you away," Derik said.

"I'm glad she protected me. I would never want to leave my home. I would rather stay in the cellar than live with the Walkers," Aryan said resolutely.

Derik sniffed.

"Are you okay, Brother? Is something wrong?"

Derik turned on the cold, stone floor. "No, a little dirt got into my nose is all. Mother would never have sent you down the Walker's path. Now get some sleep. We are close to getting the cure. I feel it in my soul."

# Phase 3

Aryan didn't bother trying to move the ripped piece of fabric that flapped in the breeze against his hand. His entire body ached from so much walking and sleeping in caves. His dry lips thirsted for water, but the Southland was parched and windy. Two days had passed without finding a spring of water and no rain fell in the south skies. He listened for his brother's footsteps ahead of him. He knew that he too was tired and thirsty because his steps also staggered along the dry ground. The darkness engulfed them both, yet they continued to meander forward.

"It's up here!" Derik shouted. "I feel it in my soul. The biggest One Tree is just ahead, and I know Mother's pregnancy root will be found growing next to it. We will dig it up and go straight back home."

"I can barely see you," Aryan cried.

"The clouds cover the sky," Derik replied.

"But there is never rain—only weeks and weeks of cloudy skies. I want to leave this place! I want to see Mother! I want to see Mother! I want to see Mother!" Aryan felt tears begin to wet his cheeks. He wanted to rub his eyes, but he knew his brother would be angry. The eyes could become easily burned by the lingering rays of the Southland sun.

But he thought it was too late for him, for they had been hurting for many days now.

He heard his brother's footsteps stop.

"Listen to me, Aryan. I promise. The root is just up ahead. Mother needs us to do this. She told me not to bring you home until the cure was found. She said we were both strong enough to finish this quest. You are younger and weaker than me. I see that you are tired. But you have more strength of heart than anyone I know. You can do this. Mother will be so pleased. The lives of our two new siblings are counting on us."

Aryan knew his brother was right. They needed to find the root to save the twins that Mother now carried. He nodded his head. "Yes, you are right. We must find the cure," he said with determination. "And when we return home, Ryun will have died. I won't have to be locked in the cellar anymore. We can keep the door open, and maybe Mother will sneak into my room and stroke my hair like she once did."

Aryan waited for his brother's reply. He could imagine his blue eyes contemplating his words.

"Yes, I believe you are right. The time has come. I am sure the Walkers weep for Ryun. He walks in eternity now. When we get home, the cellar will no longer have to be locked. Mother will want to stroke your hair and whisper her prayers. I know she cried many nights when she couldn't see you anymore."

"No, she cried over you—because you had become a man," Aryan insisted.

"No, Brother. She cried for you," Derik said. "Now let us continue our walk."

## Phase 4

Aryan felt his knees buckle. His legs could no longer carry the weight of his body. His lips and eyes were dried shut. The Southland winds cruelly beat across his face carrying grains of sand that scratched his cheeks. Several of the strips of dirty fabric fell from his body, but he no longer bothered trying to tighten them. The sun hid from the sky. Everything was black. The only color he saw was his brother's blue eyes fastened to his memory like a promise of future joy.

He heard the footsteps in front of him stop. "Brother! Go on without me. I can go no further!"

"It is as I said!" Derik exclaimed. "I have found the biggest One Tree in all of the Southland. And I see Mother's roots springing up all around it. Just a little further. Hurry! Crawl toward the sound of my voice. There is shade under the great branches."

Aryan listened to his brother calling out. He crawled on his elbows and knees toward his voice.

The scorched ground scraped against his legs and arms, but he no longer cared. He only thought of going home to the open door of the cellar. His mother could go in now and stroke his hair.

"You made it!" his brother said. "Feel the trunk of the tree. It is massive!"

Aryan pushed up from his elbows and hugged the tree, clasping his hands tightly against the bark. The tree was wide, and his arms spread out like the wings of the great Lion Eagles that fly free in the morning skies. "I feel it! We are here!"

"Now, you rest under the tree. Try to sleep. I will get plenty of Mother's pregnancy root. Then I am going to search for water. When I get back, we will quench our thirst and rest some more. Then we will be revived enough to journey home. Mother will be so happy to see us. She will have her family back again."

Aryan thought of the twins in his mother's belly. "Yes, Mother will have her whole family together." He couldn't help but smile. His dry lips peeled open. "And she will no longer have need to cry. In fact, I can see her smiling at us."

"Yes," Derik said. "She is smiling at you. She is stroking your hair. And she is whispering prayers over you. You are sleeping now in your bed. And I am finishing up the evening chores. I take my time because I know Mother likes to pet you to sleep. Do you feel it? She is petting you now."

Aryan's grin widened. "Yes, I feel it." He stopped. "I can hear her prayers too!"

"What is she saying?"

"She is praying that I find the One Tree, for He will take me Home."

"And we have found it!"

"No, this is Another One Tree. He is the Joy."

"I don't understand," Derik said. "Who is the joy?"

"When I slept in the cellar and listened to the Walkers cry out, I heard both sadness and joy as one of their own walked into eternity. He is the joy I heard. His door is always opened to anyone who seeks Him. He is never hidden, and—look! There is water all around Him!"

"You see water?" Derik asked confused.

"Yes, I see water streaming around the One Tree like waves. And light! So much light shining from Him. And there are people and kids. They are dancing and playing! I want to go to them! Derik, can I go to them?"

"But where? I don't see them," Derik said, looking around the Southland. It was mid-afternoon and the hot summer sun had faded to a soft autumn glow.

Aryan clung onto the One Tree as he tried to look over his shoulder toward his brother's voice. He saw only darkness. He returned his gaze to the One Tree and rested his cheek against the smooth bark. The One Tree shone brightly. And the water glistened blue like his brother's eyes. And the clothing of the people smelled clean and radiated with color. He wanted to go to them. "And look! It is Ryun! I see him. He is waving to me. He wants to play. Derik! Derik! Can I go to him? Please!"

"Yes, but what should I tell Mother? She will want to know why you did not return home."

Aryan spoke but kept his cheek against the bark of the One Tree. His torso pressed up against it, and he embraced as much of it as he could in his outstretched arms. "Tell her that I finally heard her prayers. Tell her that I have found the place she wanted me to find. Tell her that I met the Cure."

Derik said nothing. Aryan knew his brother was considering his words, but he didn't want to wait anymore. Ryun beckoned for him to join him, so they could play. Aryan finally got up from the tree, leaving the filthy strips of fabric behind. He was ready to go Home.

Derik watched his brother's lifeless body collapse onto the ground. The weight Derik had carried these several months finally lifted. He reached into the folds of his filthy, tattered tunic and pulled out the flagon of water his father had forced him to carry. He had refused it at first, but now his shaking hands ripped off the lid. He brought the tip of the bottle to his lips and drank deeply. He poured every ounce of liquid down his throat. The moisture soothed his parched mouth and revived his soul. He had finished his mother's quest. He had brought Aryan Home.

## Epilogue

Derik walked into the clearing of his father's land. The cool breeze of autumn greeted him knowingly. Before coming home, he had jumped into the first lake he saw when entering the Northland. The lake absorbed the gathered grime on his musty clothes he had been carrying in a satchel, and he walked away wetter yet lighter. After his brother had died, he untangled the dirty strips of cloth he wore on his body to protect against contracting the Walking Disease. He laid them on his brother's decaying body before burning everything within a perimeter of assembled stones. He buried the ashes under the large One Tree they found deep in the Southland. His brother deserved to rest under the biggest tree in all the lands. He had died fighting to return Home.

Derik walked past the rows of freshly turned soil. The harvest had finished. His father had done all the work without help. It was a difficult time for all of them. He heard a baby's cry in the distance. He looked to the porch framing the front of his family's house. He could see his mother. She held a baby in her arms. He tried to hide from her view, vying for a moment longer before having to speak with her. But she must have sensed his presence. She shielded the sun from her eyes and gazed his way. When she spotted him, she cried out over the baby's cries. She ran down the steps with the baby tightly in her arms and began to run across the field. His father must have heard her cry because he exited the tool shed and began to race across the field after her.

"Don't touch him, Lenora! Just wait so I can see him!" his father yelled.

"No, Dustin! I must see my son!" she yelled without yielding her steps.

Derik stopped walking and watched his father run in desperation past his mother. His father caught up to him first and stood with his arms spread like a wall blocking his mother's view. "Lenora, stop right now. Let me look at him first to see if there are signs of the disease."

She finally halted her run, waiting only a few feet behind her husband. "Derik knew better," she insisted. "I told him not to touch his brother. *Only use his words to soothe Aryan*, I told him." The baby fussed in her arms. She instinctively began to rock her arms side to side to quiet her cries.

"I understand, but let me just check to make sure. Give me a moment," his father said gently.

She nodded her head. Her eyes were red, and her cheeks were streaked with tears. She tried to calm her heated breaths.

His father turned back to him. "How are you doing, Son?"

"I am fine, Father. I'm glad to be home. I checked all over. No lesions or dryness. I made sure not to touch him. I think he got used to being alone toward the end."

"Lift up your shirt and turn around. They start on the neck usually."

Derik turned around and lifted his shirt over his head. He waited, feeling his father's breath on his back.

"Okay, put your shirt back on. There is nothing on you."

Derik pulled his shirt back over his head and faced his mother. He wanted to hug her, but the habit of not touching a human soul for so many months was engrained in him. She handed the baby to his father and her cries deepened as she grabbed hold of him.

"I'm so sorry. I'm so sorry. I should have let him go to the Walker's Settlement, but I couldn't lose my boy. But then I lost both of you. I'm so sorry!"

Derik tried to hold back the tears but the days on end of watching his brother slowly die tore away at his resolve. "Mother, I did it. I did what you asked of me. I took Aryan on the quest, and he died under a large One Tree deep in the Southland. I burned his body and buried him there. He is at peace now."

He felt his mother's body go limp in his arms. He tried to hold her up, but her arms shook with her sobs. "My Aryan! I wanted to go with him. I would have taken him to the Walker's Settlement. I would have hugged him each night under the stars and stroked his hair until he fell asleep. My boy! My boy! My boy! I should have gone with you!"

"Son, come hold your sister for me," his father said.

Derik got up from the ground and walked to his father. Gently, his father placed the now calm baby into Derik's arms. His father then fell to his knees onto the ground in front of his wife and engulfed her in his arms. They both wept.

"Lenora, there was nothing you could have done. If you would have contracted the Walking Disease, Aydan and Arella would have died too. Look," he said pointing to Derik who was holding a now sleeping baby. "Arella is healthy. And Aydan sleeps soundly in his crib after you lulled him to sleep with your touch."

His mother released herself from her husband's arms, not wanting to be consoled. She leaned her face onto the ground and pressed her cheek against the dark soil. "I know, but it still hurts. My boy! If I would have known that day would be the last I would ever get to touch him, I would have held on longer!"

"Don't cry, Mother," Derik said softly, not wanting to wake Arella. "I wish you could have heard Aryan. He was so excited to leave. He had been completely blind for almost a month, but suddenly he saw color again. And he saw the One Tree you prayed about. He heard you, Mother! He heard your voice praying over him."

His mother lifted her head from the ground. The soft soil clung to her face. "He heard my prayers?"

Derik nodded. "Yes, and he was so excited to go. He saw Ryun playing. And bright lights and water surrounding the One Tree. He told me to tell you that he found the place you wanted him to find. He found the Cure. He is Home."

Lenora covered her face with her hands and began to weep. Her voice rose in sadness and her wails echoed across the Northland. Her husband gently brought her back into his embrace. Derik stood holding his baby sister against his chest and listened to his mother mourn. The breeze pulled at the sadness, and a hint of joy lifted into the fading rays of the autumn sun. He heard another cry coming from the house. Baby Aydan was awake, and he needed his mother. Their family was together again, and Aryan's memory would live on in the stories his father, mother and brother would tell the twins.

# Devotional Study

As I reread this story, tears streak my face and drip from my chin. As a mother, if my child was in pain, I would instantly do everything in my power to ease the pain. I would have gone to the Walkers Settlement with my child in a heartbeat. Life is brief. Eternity is forever. Love is more valuable than anything. However, if I had babies in my womb, I'm now responsible for two other lives. This reminds me of when my identical twin sister almost died in a car accident. We lived in different cities, but God woke me up with a terrible pain in my abdomen. The interesting thing about the situation was that I felt the pain, but it didn't hurt. I knew something was seriously wrong, so I checked on my nine-month-old firstborn. He was fine, but I decided to bring him to bed with me. That's when I heard the phone ring. It was my sister's husband telling me that she was being airlifted by helicopter to a large hospital. They didn't know if she was going to make it.

When I finally got to the hospital, I could barely be there for my twin. My baby was breastfed and wouldn't take a bottle well. Babies weren't allowed in the hospital rooms. I had to ask family and friends to watch him for just enough time to see her. If I didn't have a baby, I wouldn't have left her room day or night, but now I was responsible for another who needed me. It is one of the worst predicaments to be in. God did, however, redeem that situation by allowing me to be there for her in another surgery she had (story can be found in my book, *Following God Across the Page*). The only hope I can gain from situations like these is that we have a Father in Heaven Who loves us and our loved ones more than we can fathom. And He has a Home for us in Heaven where there will be no more pain. We will be in complete peace and joy because we will be in the Presence of God. This broken life is brief, but thank God the Cure, Jesus Christ, has given us access to eternity placed in our hearts!

> "*God has planted eternity in the human heart…*" (Ecclesiastes 3:11 NLT).

Just as a side note, every section of the story starts with the name "Ayran." However, the final section starts with his brother's name, Derik. The readers finally get to see from his point of view and the points of view of his parents. The dramatic irony is finally over, and the family can live in full truth once more.

## Reflection Questions

Have you ever been caught in a proverbial *rock and a hard place*? What did if feel like to face two unfavorable and opposing circumstances? Were you able to give the situation to God? Did God redeem the situation or give you understanding about it?

# Five Literary Devices

1. **<u>Dramatic Irony:</u>** The audience of a story is aware of circumstances and speeches outside the understanding of the story's characters.

**Short Story:** The audience becomes aware that Aryan has the Walking Disease because they can see from an adult perspective. They understand that his friend, Ryun, got the disease and was banished. They see him locked in a cellar not because his older brother, Derik, became a man, but because Aryan was infected. They see that he is losing his sight toward the end of the story, and he must cover himself to hide his lesions. Finally, they understand that the "quest" they were on was to help him die with family—at least his brother.

**Bible:** The *Book of Job* is one of dramatic irony. The readers overhear God's conversation with Satan about Job being the most righteous man alive. They also know that God has given Satan permission to put Job through great affliction, losing his family, wife, wealth and health. Job doesn't understand why all the tragedy has befallen him. He didn't get the memo from Heaven. However, the readers understand that God is testing him, and they are rooting for him to overcome his struggle and receive his double blessing by staying faithful to God even during intense adversity.

2. **Foreshadowing:** A hint of future events using subtle similarities.

**Short Story:** "But his brother was no longer by his side, forcing the perfume of the dead to now share his bed."

**Bible:** *"All right,' Jesus replied. 'Destroy this temple, and in three days I will raise it up'"* (John 2:19 NLT).

3. **Metaphor:** A comparison between two seemingly unlike things.

**Short Story:** "She is praying that I find the One Tree, for He will take me Home."

**Bible:** *"The tongue also is a fire, a world of evil among the parts of the body. It corrupts the whole body, sets the whole course of one's life on fire, and is itself set on fire by hell"* (James 3:6 NIV).

4. **Paradox:** Combines two contradicting ideas to create a logical and deeper meaning.

**Short Story:** "Their sad howls rang of joy—sadness for the life lost and joy for the pain ended."

**Bible:** *"And He sat down, called the twelve, and said to them, 'If anyone desires to be first, he shall be last of all and servant of all'"* Mark 9:35 NKJV).

5. **Repetition:** Repeating a word or phrase to show emphasis.

**Short Story:** "I want to leave this place! I want to see Mother! I want to see Mother! I want to see Mother!"

**Bible:** *"Each one of the four living beings had six wings. They had eyes all over them, inside and out. Day and night they never stop saying, "Holy, holy, holy is the Lord God, the All-powerful One. He is the One Who was and Who is and Who is to come"* (Revelation 4:8 NLV).

# A WRITER'S TOLL

His hands shook. Where was his brandy? He patted his trousers. Nothing. He had been just about to take a drink, but the air suddenly lacked life. The atmosphere chilled his skin. A dream. Or maybe another hallucination. He tried to stand up, but his feet were fastened to the chair.

*"To the moaning and the groaning* … My cousin, have you locked me up again?" he shouted.

"Your cousin, you say? Tell me about her," a woman's voice sounded.

He didn't recognize the accent. "Who are you? Where am I? Why can't I see?"

"You are still in Virginia. We must keep the room dark to minimize visual stimuli. I just have a couple of questions for you. It won't take long. Then we will bring you back to what you were doing before. What were you doing?"

"I was drinking my brandy!" he yelled. "Why can't I stand?"

"You must stay seated if you want to go back," the voice clanged. "Were you in your aunt's home?"

"I demand an explanation! I will not answer any further questions!"

"That's too bad. You will not remember any of our conversation. It will be disappointing to go through all this work and not get to know you a little more."

"Why would anyone want to know me?"

The voice paused. Her breath vibrated like tinkling bells. A chair scraped against the concrete floor, and her rapid breathing drew closer.

"They required that I not say anything except ask my questions to verify the facts. I was hoping this day would come; and when it did, they requested the expert. Me."

"Expert of what?"

"You, of course."

"Me?"

"How about this?" she dinged. "We will have a question-and-answer game. I will answer one of your questions, and you will answer one of mine."

He brushed his arm across his parched mouth. He wished he would have taken his second drink of brandy. "I'm first. Where am I?"

"You are in Virginia."

"That is not what I meant!"

"Well, you are the writer, aren't you? Ask more specifically. My turn. What have you written so far?"

"How do you know I'm a writer?" he inquired.

"If you are not going to play our question-and-answer game correctly, we will not play at all."

"Only two books of poetry. They did poorly. I'm surprised you know them."

"I know much more than that," she clinked a laugh.

He considered her words "What exactly does this facility do?"

"We take famous people for brief moments to verify facts. What are you writing currently?"

"I don't know," he answered.

"Impossible!" the voice rang out. "You, the literary genius, have nothing? That is no answer!"

He held up his hands. "No, it is true. I never know until it knocks into me. Then I must scribble as fast as my hands allow. It is like trying to capture a fading vision before it vanishes."

"Very interesting!" the woman's voice pealed.

He thought and asked, "How is it that you know more about me than I do?"

"Now that is a question from the master! I know everything about you because I've spent my life studying you. When this writing vision comes to you, is it fully complete like a gift of words?"

He shook his head. "No, I gain only a feeling .... a mere glimpse that I must wrestle to reveal. It can take days or weeks to grasp the entirety of it. It is quite laborious."

"How wonderful," she jingled.

"Does everyone know my work?" he asked.

"Everyone who matters. We teach you. We study you. Your writings changed literature as we know it! And I should know. I am the expert."

"Yes, so you have mentioned." He wrung his hands together and felt the callouses from the hours of writing with his quill pen. "I am a man of no significance, I assure you."

"You are a renowned insignificant!" the voice resounded.

His hands fell to his knees. "That is a paradox!"

"Of course, the great writer would reference a literary device! Even when speaking, you write!" the voice boomed.

The chair scooted itself a touch closer to him, and the voice chimed near his ear.

"Your struggle with words is what makes your life and writing so very intriguing. Your angst is something we no longer experience. Our lives are quite boring and easy now," her voice resonated.

"Easy," he rasped.

A bell signaled. "Oh no!" the woman's voice tolled. "You are about to be sent back. I am not supposed to do this, but please, give me your signature on this page."

"What is it?" he asked.

"It is your life's work," she dinged. Her breath tickled his mustache. She placed the book on his lap. "Here, take my pen and sign it quickly before you leave. Sign it to me. My name is Campana—C.A.M.P.A.N.A." She dinged each letter in consecutive order.

He placed his hand on the book feeling its thickness. His life's work. Done. No wrestling. No striving. Given freely without a fight. A life of both renown and ease. He scribbled his signature and held up the pen. "A pen, you say. I like it."

"Regrettably, you must give it back. They say if you bring anything back from our time, it will trigger your memories."

"I will give it to you." He clenched the pen with his fist and stabbed it into the breath of the voice, silencing the infuriating cadence as sweet sounds of moaning and groaning choked it out.

He dropped the pen and clutched the book in his desperate arms.

His eyes opened. His tumbler stumbled across the wooden floor, spilling the brandy. Was it another cruel dream? Had fate tricked him again? He loosened the grasp of one hand and pounded his chest twice. *Thump. Thump.* A book indeed. A book! A large volume of his own work! He gripped his life's work with trembling fingers and brought it to view. He beamed over the hardcover like a father over his newborn son and gently wiped the splattered blood with his sleeve. "The Complete Works of Edgar Allan

Poe," he whispered in awe. "I am a writer who will never have to wrestle words again."

## Devotional Study

I wrote this short story to submit to an online flash fiction publisher. I knew when I kept out the words, "she said," the editor would either understand my use of literary device or not. I replaced all the "said" words of the woman character with words that alluded to bells ringing, hinting at Edgar Allen Poe's famous poem, "The Bells," to irritate the reader until she/he discovered that the famous author mentioned was, indeed, Edgar Allen Poe. Clarity would trigger and then, hopefully, produce intrigue and a good laugh. My allusion to his poem describing the irritating sounds of the bells in the city would finally become clear. If the editor didn't get that I was alluding to his poem, my short story would certainly be rejected. As a creative, I took the chance. You have to know the rules to break the rules, and I broke a big one to cause irritation to the reader. The editor did reject my short story and wrote to me plainly that I should use "she said" more. She didn't get the literary device, but I was pleased to know that my literary device of allusion worked. I accomplished irritating her since my literary device of allusion had alluded her.

I wrote this story because as a writer, I wrestle with words. Specifically, as a Christian writer, I feel like

Jacob wrestling with the Angel of the Lord when I sit down at the computer (Genesis 32:22-32). God wants to give me deeper revelation, but to receive it, I must wrestle with Him (of sorts) in meditation as I type out His thoughts and make them my own, so I can share them with others. Then, I receive greater spiritual wisdom as my flesh breaks (another allusion to Jacob's wrenched hip). My writing is what grows and matures me. My wrestling is what makes me spiritually stronger. If God would have offered me my life's work twenty-years ago, and I knew how much difficulty, discouragement and rejection I would face and how much time, money and determination I would have to give, I might have taken the offer. But I am so thankful now for the obstacles along the way because they made me the strong, wise and resilient person I am today. And I still have more to learn, more to grow and more to write!

> *"Not only so, but we also glory in our sufferings, because we know that suffering produces perseverance; perseverance, character; and character, hope. And hope does not put us to shame, because God's love has been poured out into our hearts through the Holy Spirit, who has been given to us"* (Romans 5:3-5 NIV).

## Reflection Questions

Can you think of a few obstacles that you have faced and overcome? How did those difficulties make you stronger and wiser? Was God able to use those difficult times for His greater good? Is there something you are wrestling with currently that has you relying on God's strength in your life?

## Five Literary Devices

1. **Allusion:** Is an indirect reference to someone or something that can be understood in a personal or cultural context.

**Short Story:** "The chair scooted itself a touch closer to him, and the voice chimed near his ear."

**Bible:** *"Jesus said to them, 'Most assuredly, I say to you, before Abraham was, I AM'"* (John 8:58 NKJV).

2. **Epigraph:** A short quotation toward the beginning of a section of writing with the aim of signifying the theme.

**Short Story:** *"To the moaning and the groaning*...My cousin, have you locked me up again?" This is the first part of the last line of Edgar Allan Poe's poem, "The Bells." I'm using it as a theme that from my personal study of his life, I believe he would take the manuscript of his life's work because of a lack of integrity and his many damaging life choices.

**Bible:** *"Certainly not! Indeed, let God be true but every man a liar. As it is written: 'That You may be justified in Your words, And may overcome when You are judged'"* (Romans 3:4 NKJV). Paul opened this section of Scripture with a quote from the Old

Testament referencing Psalm 51:4 to explain the truth that God does not lie, and He is blameless when He makes judgments."

3. **Onomatopoeia:** Words that represent the sound they make.

**Short Story:** "He loosened the grasp of one hand and pounded his chest twice. *Thump. Thump.* A book, indeed. A book!"

**Bible:** *"And God said to Moses, 'I am Yahweh—the LORD. I appeared to Abraham, to Isaac, and to Jacob as El-Shaddai—"God Almighty"—but I did not reveal my name, Yahweh, to them'"* (Exodus 6:2-3 NLT). The name *Yahweh* emulates the sound of the breath of God. *Yah* is the inhale. *Wey* is the exhale. There are more examples of onomatopoeia in the original Biblical languages of Hebrew, Aramaic and Greek.

4. **Onomastics:** Names that have meaning in the original language that relate to the person's character.

**Short Story:** "'Here, take my pen and sign it quickly before you leave. Sign it to me. My name is Campana—C.A.M.P.A.N.A.' She dinged each letter in consecutive order." The name, "Campana," means *bell ringer* in Latin.

**Bible:** *"I appeal to you for my son Onesimus, whom I have begotten while in my chains, who once was unprofitable to you, but now is profitable to you and to me" (Philemon 1:10-11 NKJV).* The name, "Onesimus," means *profitable* in Greek.

5. **Oxymoron:** Combines two contradictory words to offer meaningful insight.

**Short Story:** "'You are a renowned insignificant!' the voice resounded." *Renowned* and *insignificant* are opposites, but the deeper truth is that he will be more famous when he's dead.

**Bible:** *"Therefore, I urge you, brothers and sisters, in view of God's mercy, to offer your bodies as a living sacrifice, holy and pleasing to God—this is your true and proper worship"* (Romans 12:1 NIV). A sacrifice signifies death and cannot be living, but the literary device gives us a deeper meaning that we should live our lives dead to our sinful selves and alive in Christ.

# ONE WAY UP

The breath within her halted as her body floated lifelessly in currents of the arid compound explosion. The numbing noise beat her eardrums to submission. For a moment, she thought she would stay in the sordid status for unceasing suspension—a time of infinite torment. Finally, her body crunched onto the concrete like a bird flying into thick glass. No shattering, though. Stunned but awake. She still lived; all bones were intact but dying would be easier. Hot oxygen filled her lungs once more. Hope seemed too elusive to grasp, but the adrenaline pumping through her veins vexed her to advance.

It happened all at once, this madness. Aliens, demons, hybrids of some sort—all fighting humans. Men and women wearing camouflage with flailing limbs as blood splayed across their uniforms and USA-patched sleeves, called to duty and to dying, and most were fleeing. The monsters hunched over the soldiers like falling mountains eager to crush them.

*Where were the civilians like her? Normal men and women and children. Dead? Hidden? Safe? No thoughts. Just run. Get to a place with less screams, less blood, less madness.*

An alien haunted her side view. Anger streaked across his face. Hate thundered even more. His appearance didn't simply send shivers down her spine. Her entire body wanted to freeze with fear.

She would have laughed at the cliché of words in earlier days as an English major earning her Master of Arts Degree. Her greatest fear only a week ago was getting a low grade for a course or not having enough money for rent. How easy those days now seemed since the monsters revealed themselves. No spaceships. No warning. They simply appeared as if they were already on earth dwelling among them unseen.

The words "steal, kill and destroy," rang through her mind like the shockwave of the bomb that flung her to the ground. Sounded familiar. Maybe from the college Bible club her roommate dragged her to. God? No thanks. His Son coming to Earth? It all sounded ridiculous at the time. Now surrounded by monsters the prospect of a Savior sounded less preposterous. A sharp snarl scraped behind her. *Run faster.* This enemy's shadow usurped her on every level. No win in the books for the undervalued humans who now seemed like mere bugs. The bugs had not scared and scattered. The monsters had no agenda but to terminate. At first, she thought it was a political ploy but listened to the news as heads of state all over the world succumbed to invasion. Famous people too. The list of dead names multiplied like rocks being hurled in a hurricane from the quiet yards of island homes. The hurricane must have ripped through the news too as the monsters silenced them.

A college student wouldn't survive this apocalypse if the rich and famous fell. Yet, suddenly, she sensed a clearing in the morbid mayhem that smiled on the mess. Not a Savior but maybe a way out. The beast chasing her tore up another victim that ran just behind her. She felt the victim's blood splash against the back of her shirt. It gave her just enough time to follow the civilians who ran with intuition. What did they know that she didn't? They silently slipped into this underground holding area. No aliens. Only people running into the quieter shadows. The light evaporated to a hazy dusk. The bombings blared less. A large, thick gate blocked the way, but a man pulled out a key and unlocked it. He held the metal door open as the civilians and some soldiers passed through the slim entrance. He was just about to shut the door.

"Let me in!" she screamed.

He looked at her and shook his head. "You don't have access."

"But you just let all those people in with your key. Would you leave me behind with monsters killing everyone?"

"They asked to enter beforehand," he said simply.

"I'm asking now!"

He looked beyond her to the blood-stained devastation. "I will let you in, but the hope you are looking for is not down here."

He held the door open briefly, and she glided in. What did he mean there was no hope down here? He had just let dozens of people in. This place had to be safer than outside. The man locked the door behind her and ran forward. The dark atmosphere caused her pupils to fully dilate. She needed to find the man and the others. Where had they gone? Something was different about them. They rushed with purpose, and confusion didn't distort their faces. They had some secret of safety.

Before she could look for them, she stepped several feet back and gaped. Unspoiled uniforms were working on a massive wall-lined machine barely lit up with dangling light bulbs hanging from long wires connected to the high ceiling. The soldiers moved with knowledge and efficiency. She covered her mouth to mute her scream. Women strapped to neo-electric chairs lined the angular, dense walls to the right of the machine. Black disks attached to their breasts sucked down milk, and the white fluid mixed with a concoction of chemicals pumped through hoses into the machine. Buttons on the machine glowed as a pressed uniform soldier took out a vile of tainted white liquid and pressed it into a weapon she had never seen before.

The woman's legs were immobile for a moment as her mind computed but could not calculate what she beheld.

"It's chemical warfare," a voice said behind her. She turned. It was the man with the key.

"It's their final attempt to kill the demons, but you can't kill what's not living."

"Why breast milk?" she asked abhorred.

"It makes the demons vanish. They think if they mix deathly chemicals with it, the mixture will kill them."

"Will it work?" she asked, hopefully.

Again, he shook his head. "You can't fight powers of darkness with flesh and blood. It will destroy the world."

"And us?"

He looked back toward the gate he had opened. "The world is already being destroyed."

He gazed at her for several seconds. "The Way was given to you many times, and you dismissed it. You didn't ask for the Way because you didn't see your need."

"I see my need now!"

"Your need for a Savior or your need for a way out?"

"Either will work!" she exclaimed.

"That's not how this works. You must want the Savior as your Way out."

"Fine, what do I need to do?"

"You accept the fact that you are a sinner, repent and ask for the salvation gifted to you by God's Son, Jesus."

She felt uncomfortable with his words. She lived a good life. She didn't hurt people. She had no regrets and nothing to be sorry for. Suddenly, she saw the way out. The civilians and the few soldiers were climbing up steep ladders into holes that led up. She could see light streaming from the openings. That's the secret they knew. That was the way out. The government must have saved an oasis knowing this was going to happen, and only a few knew about it. Now she knew. She didn't need to talk to this key-keeper anymore. She saw the way out.

She didn't bother talking to the man. She ran to the closest ladder that lined the walls opposite of the chemical-milk machine. She grabbed hold of the first rung of the ladder. She could feel the light and warmth on her face already. She would make it. Just a college student, and she found the way out. The government had kept the escape quiet. Probably for the prestigious people of the world. Still it didn't make sense that so many famous and rich people died. Wouldn't they have known? She grabbed rung after rung until she was at the entrance to the circular hole in the ceiling. She could see the oasis. Her eyes beheld beauty. Flower-lined meadows.

Light radiating everywhere but not from a sun that she could see. People laughing. Kids playing. Joy. Love. Peace. She could sense it all. She just needed to get in.

But then she noticed the way was blocked. Iron rods halted her entrance.

"Why are you blocked?" she demanded of the round exit from the ruin below. "I saw dozens of people enter through. Why are you stopping me from entering?" She looked to her left. "Fine, I will go to another one." She quickly made her way down the long ladder and ran to the one next to it. She climbed up every rail and again she saw the light and the warmth. Sensed the joy, love and peace. Again, the way was blocked.

"What is going on with you? I just saw people go through into the oasis."

The sounds from the chemical machine blared. They were done mixing their milk and chemical concoction. The uniforms were lining up to wield their chemical weapon on the enemy outside. They were about to open the gates and let the monsters in. She needed to hurry up. She slid down this ladder and went to the next one. Out of breath, she crawled up. Again, the way was blocked.

"Why can I get through you?" she screamed at the opening. Suddenly, a sign appeared above the entrance. It had all the world's religions written on it. As she read each one, a punch of fear hit her gut. Then the key-keeper on the other side of the entrance looked at her. He had sadness on his face though the atmosphere around him was saturated with joy. He shook his head. "Those religions won't help you."

"No religion can help me! I just need a way out!"

"I offered you the Way, and you discarded it," he said.

"No, you didn't. You tried to hide these ladders and openings to this oasis from me."

He shook his head again. "I offered you the true Way, and you didn't take it. You never accepted Him."

"What is this Way? Some Jesus? Some Cross?"

The gate below was open now, and gunfire echoed through the underground lab. She held onto the ladder and looked behind her. The soldiers were shooting monsters. They would disappear, but the soldier shooting instantly screamed out in pain and fell in convulsions. They were dying. The soldiers. The deadly chemicals saturated the air, and she began to cough. "Let me in!"

He shook his head one final time. "The entrance is closing now. I will leave you with these final words. 'Jesus is the Way and the Truth and the Life. No one comes to the Father except through

Him.' I tried to help you find the Way, but you wouldn't accept Him. I am sorry. I did all I could do, but the free will choice was yours."

Then the lights of the entrance went black. The sense of joy, love and peace vanished, leaving her in terror. She looked behind her and coughed again, but this time blood wetted her mouth. The chemicals acted quickly. The soldiers were all dead. The demons gone, but they fulfilled their purpose. They killed the humans by tricking them into killing each other. She looked back at the blocked entrance. The Way out was not a hole in the ceiling. It was God in the flesh, and she would not accept Him.

## Devotional Study

This is the first time I've ever written about a dream I had in fiction form. I was the girl in this dream, and when I woke up, I was upset at God. I felt so hopeless. I told Him that I have been a Christian since I was fifteen years old. Over thirty years now. I accepted the Way and wrote about Him in over forty books. Why did He have me dream this terrifying experience of being locked out of His Presence? He explained that this is what will happen to many people who do not accept the Messiah, our only connection to God. They will live experiencing the hopelessness I felt. It saddened me and gave me greater passion to continue to write and talk about Jesus even though I feel like no one is listening and if they are listening, they don't hear or care. I dream frequently in story form, but I've never been on the other side of salvation since I was fifteen years old. This dream gave me grave insight into the importance of sharing the Good News of Jesus Christ.

I almost wrote this short story in first person because it was me in the dream, and I have never published a story in first person. I like third person because I can be in the minds of my characters without actually being them. However, when I started writing, I couldn't write it in first person. I didn't want to be this girl. I could experience her in third person, but I would not use the words "I" and "me." Also, the milk in the dream seems odd, but I have dreamed about milk before and looked up its prophetic meaning years ago. Prophet James Goll explains in his book, *Dream Language*, that milk represents, "Foundational truth and nourishment." So, these soldiers were taking truth but tainting it. They were taking organic nourishment and mixing it with human-devised chemicals. Instead of seeking the Truth, they were trying to create their own truth. It is sad to think that we have the gift of salvation, but instead of accepting it, people will go to great lengths to find their own counterfeit salvation, which ended up costing them their lives and was exactly what the enemy wanted.

> *"Jesus answered, 'I am the way and the truth and the life. No one comes to the Father except through me'"* (John 14:6 NIV).

## Reflection Questions

How old were you when you received Jesus Christ as your Lord and Savior? Did you feel a difference, like looking through new eyes? Have you shared the Good News of Jesus Christ with others, including family and friends? Does your life reflect the love of Jesus to the people around you?

# Five Literary Devices

1. **Allegory:** A literary work that represents something else.

**Short Story:** This short story is a science fiction allegorical work representing our ability to accept or reject the Gospel. The hole in the ceiling leading to the Oasis (Heaven) is a symbol of Jesus being the only Way out. The girl represents our individual free will choice to accept Jesus or not. The monsters represent Satan and his demons and their absolute evil desire to keep us from reaching Heaven. The key-keeper represents Christians who know the Way out and offer this free gift to others. The world ending represents the eventual death of this world, and the Oasis is the birth of a New Earth (Revelation 21).

**Bible:** Jesus used many allegorical parables. One is "The Parable of the Weeds" to describe the Kingdom of Heaven (Matthew 13:24-30). A man planted good seeds in his field, but the enemy planted weeds while everyone slept. The servants asked if they should pull up the weeds, but the man told them not to because they would accidentally pull up the wheat too. The wheat and weeds would grow together until the harvest and then the harvesters would separate them. In this allegory, the one who sowed the seeds is Jesus. The good seeds are the people who accepted Jesus as their Savior. The bad seeds are the people who have not. The harvest is the end of this age, and the harvesters are angels.

2. **Apostrophe:** A form of personification where the character speaks to an inanimate object.

**Short Story:** "Why are you blocked?' she demanded of the round exit from the ruin below. 'I saw dozens of people enter through. Why are you stopping me from entering?' She looked to her left. 'Fine, I will go to another one.'"

**Bible:** *"Sing, O heavens, for the LORD has done this wondrous thing. Shout for joy, O depths of the earth! Break into song, O mountains and forests and every tree! For the LORD has redeemed Jacob and is glorified in Israel"* (Isaiah 44:23 NLT).

3. **Flashback:** Engages interest in the narrative by detailing background information of a character.

**Short Story:** "She would have laughed at the cliché of words in earlier days as an English major earning her Master of Arts Degree. Her greatest fear only a week ago was getting a low grade for a course or not having enough money for rent. How easy those days now felt since the monsters revealed themselves."

**Bible:** *"After Joshua sent the people away, each of the tribes left to take possession of the land allotted to them. And the Israelites served the LORD throughout the lifetime of Joshua and the leaders who outlived him—those who had seen all the great things the LORD had done for Israel"* (Judges 2:6-7 NLT). Joshua has already died (Judges 1:1), but the writer is reminding the readers of all the great things God accomplished for the people to gain their land through Joshua's leadership. They didn't fully obey God after Joshua's death by not casting out the locals of the lands, so God warned them that those who they did not drive out would be thorns in their side (Judges 2:3). But for now, it was time to move on and possess the land that Joshua, in obedience to God, led them to.

4. **Idiom:** An expression that is attached to a specific language and culture.

**Short Story:** "His appearance didn't simply *send shivers down her spine.* Her entire body wanted to freeze with fear."

**Bible:** *"And when we all had fallen to the ground, I heard a voice speaking to me and saying in the Hebrew language, 'Saul, Saul, why are you persecuting Me? It is hard for you to kick against the goads'"* (Acts 26:14 NKJV). Kicking against the goads is translated in the NLT to "It is useless for you to fight against my will."

5. **Metonymy:** A type of metaphor where the thing, person or idea is not identified by its own name but by another name closely related.

**Short Story:** "I tried to help you find the Way, but you wouldn't accept Him. I am sorry. I did all I could do, but the free will choice was yours."

**Bible:** *"I am the way and the truth and the life. No one comes to the Father except through me"* (John 14:6 NIV).

# 9-HOLES

## Hole I

AN atmosphere of stillness saturated the golf course, yet the tension between the two golf partners surpassed the calm. The stillness and the tension formed the totality of life—both the good and the bad. The sun had not yet risen above the horizon. It was five in the morning, and the weather had turned cold in South Texas. The two figures could barely be seen on hole one of the golf course. No one was around anyway to notice them.

The course didn't open for another three hours. Not even the greenspeople had arrived for work yet.

"What are we doing here? I haven't been a member of the country club for over a year," Janet said.

She was a middle-aged woman with a thin body and an irritated expression. She wore black golf pants and a black golf jacket. Her clubs were in a worn golf bag resting in a pushcart. She wore a white glove on her left hand. Her wedding ring could be seen bulging out of the leather. She stared at her partner waiting for the answer.

"I want to play golf with you. There are things we need to discuss and process, and golf was always the activity that brought us together," her partner said.

Janet huffed. "I don't want to play this game with you! I feel ridiculous out here in the dark and cold. I won't be able to make a decent shot anyway. I can't even see the flag."

"Yes," her partner said. "But you know as well as I do that as long as we have been married, we have played this course. What? Twenty-four years? You know where to hit. Just hit the ball by faith."

"You make me want to laugh. You want to do an intervention on the greens? What are you going to do while I golf? Just watch me?"

"No, I want to talk with you. I'm concerned. There is something you're not handling, and it's affecting your mental and physical health."

Janet pulled back her shoulders. "I'm completely fine."

"How much weight have you lost this past year?" her partner asked.

"It is none of your business!" Janet exclaimed.

"I am your husband. I deserve to know what is going on. But I will never know unless you figure it out for yourself."

"Husband, indeed," Janet said, rolling her eyes.

"And the drinking?" her partner added. "You are drinking to cope. I see it. Your twin sister and your mother see it. You're barely making it."

Janet shoved the head of her golf club toward her partner's face. "I will have you know that the author I signed a year ago has just landed on the New York Times Best Sellers List. My literary agency is thriving."

"Yeah, I know. That's all you do is work. You no longer socialize. You used to love to throw parties. You don't visit your mother or your twin anymore. When was the last time you called your son or daughter? Just because one is married, and the other is in college doesn't mean you're not their mother anymore. They need you."

"My mother and my twin are fine. My kids are fine. You know they have enough on their plate than to deal with me too."

"Then why do they call me concerned about you?"

Janet gripped the driver at her side and grabbed for the tee in her pocket. "Let's just golf and get this game over with."

She reached down and put the tee in between the wooden markers of the tee box. Then she got behind the ball. "I really can't see anything. If I hit a house, I will poison your water and dump your body in the Gulf of Mexico."

Her partner laughed. "Strong words coming from someone I love."

Janet ignored the statement and got into her normal stance. She had been doing the same tee-off for so many years that she could probably do it blindfolded. "I can barely see the ball."

"Just hit it," her partner said. "It will find its mark."

Janet swung her club by thrusting her hips to where she believed the hole to be. Her arms followed just behind her waist. "Dang it! My club face was tilted in because I can't see the ball. It's going to be lost in the trees."

Suddenly, a thumping sound could be heard in the distance.

"I think it hit a tree," her partner said. "Maybe it pushed it back to the fairway."

"I doubt it," Janet said. "Get your flashlight from your phone. If we can't find it, I am calling it quits to this game we are playing."

## Hole 2

By the time they made it to hole two, Janet rested. She wasn't used to pushing the golf bag pushcart and walking such distances. Maybe she needed to get out more often. She was losing her strength. She once was proud of her athletic physique, but now she looked as skinny as a supermodel minus the super.

"I honestly don't know how that ball got onto the green. I hit it into the trees. Your theory was correct. It must have bounced off the large palm tree and rolled right back into the fairway," Janet said, feeling a little better about their unauthorized game. The darkness still covered the grounds, but her partner was right. She had memorized this course from hole one to hole eighteen—though she always insisted on doing only the back nine or the front nine. She had never relented to doing all eighteen holes in one day. Four hours of golf was a lot, and she looked forward to lunch and drinks afterward. But that was no more. Her membership with the country club had ended.

"I think the angels are on your side," her partner said. "I have no idea how to play golf and yet I knew."

"Huh, but you have played golf with me for over twenty-four years," Janet said with a smirk.

"Yes, I'm sorry. I play this game often."

Janet sighed "Why must you bring your faith into this game? Angelic beings? Really? They're not concerned with me and this game. Why would God care?"

Her partner turned to her, and Janet could feel the care emanating. It made her ashamed of her words.

"He cares about you. He cares about your struggle, and, yes, He cares about this game we are playing. It is important."

"Whatever you say, Husband," Janet scoffed. "Let me tee off on this second hole before the sun comes up and we get caught. We still have eight more holes to go. This one is easier. The flag is right beyond the creek. I just need to make sure not to sink my ball in the water. I'm still having trouble seeing."

"What happens if you sink it?"

"You of all people should know. I won't get par. That was your passion to never get a bogey. But you loved your birdies. You always wanted a birdie on the ninth hole. You never got it, and it drove you crazy. You wanted to show off to all your friends at the clubhouse at the last hole with a birdie. Guess it will never happen."

"You could do it. You could get the birdie at the ninth hole when the sun comes up."

Janet laughed. "I never played as well as you. I only did it to appease you and fulfill my wifely duties."

Her partner leaned back. "I don't believe that. You enjoyed playing with me. I remember you calling your twin excited that it was game day."

Janet looked away and grabbed the driver once again in her hand and took out the tee from her pocket. "Well, that was over a year ago. I haven't played since. Let me tee off, so we can hurry up and not get caught."

She placed the tee in the damp grass in her accustomed place. She just needed to get the golf ball over the creek. She hated when she sunk the ball in front of her husband. He would say nothing, but the disappointment in his face said it all. She could barely make out the water in front of her, but from years of playing she knew how hard to swing. She needed to ensure the ball lifted, so she brought the tee up a little more from the ground.

"All I have is my instinct," she said to herself. She readied and swung her hips with her arms close behind her. They heard a splash. She slammed the driver to the grass. "I knew it! I didn't get the ball high enough."

"Wait! Did you hear that skid of water? It's like the ball ricocheted across the water like a stone."

"Can't be. I've never done that before."

"Isn't there always a first time?" her partner asked.

"Let us go see," Janet said grabbing her golf bag pushcart and rolling it toward the cement walkway that led to the other side of the creek.

"Turn on the flashlight on your phone," she told her partner.

The light only gave three feet of visual, but once they got to the green, Janet saw the ball. It was only a club's distance behind the hole.

"Wow! I have never gotten a birdie on this hole. My husband would be so proud!"

"You mean *I* would be so proud," her partner said.

"Yes, I forgot, Husband. Now, let me hit this ball in. Wow! A birdie."

"Is this an easy shot?" her partner asked.

"Wouldn't you know being my husband and all," Janet snickered. She lined the ball up with the hole. She saw a slight tilt of the land to the left, so she would aim to the right side of the circle. She got her hands in position and then aligned her feet. "Nice and easy. There is a slight slope, and the grass is still damp from the morning dew." She used her shoulders, keeping her waist tight and arms straight. She gently tapped the ball, and it rolled right into the hole.

"Yes! I can't believe it!" she said, hugging her partner. "This would be grounds for a drink after the game."

"I will gladly watch you drink one. You know I stopped over a year ago."

Janet's smile faded. "You and Mom both stopped."

"And your twin. Why do you think that is?"

"That's your business, not mine. Let's move to the third hole. Time is running out."

"You want me to push your cart thingy for you?"

"No, I'll push my own weight."

## Hole 3

Calls of the indigenous ducks who made their home on the country club course finally began to sound. They were waking up as the pair of golfers made it to the third hole.

"Can you even see the flag from here?" her partner asked.

"I can't see anything, but I know there is a long fairway, and the tee green is to the left. I need to hit the ball forward with force. There are three sand traps around the tee green, so when I round the corner for my second hit, the ball will have to drop over them onto the green if I am to make par."

"This game is so complicated," her partner said.

"Well, I think *your* game is ridiculous," Janet said. "But at least I'm playing well. That is the only reason I'm still here."

"Do you want to talk about our relationship?" her partner asked.

"You mean as husband and wife until death do us part?" Janet asked. Her stomach suddenly felt sick.

"Look, I can tell you are hurting. Marriage can tear you apart, but there is something with which you are not dealing. If you don't process your pain, I fear you will slowly kill yourself."

"What do you know of it, huh? What do you know of pain?"

Her partner looked at her solemnly. "You know I've had my share of pain in this life."

Janet looked down. "Yes, I know. I am sorry."

"But the good times eventually come again if you let them, but you have to let go."

"I have let go!" Janet yelled.

Her partner thought. "No, there is obviously something you are holding onto, and it is poisoning your life."

Janet looked back at the fairway. "This will be impossible to make par in the dark. Just letting you know that I will get a bogey or even a double bogey. Or I may just mess the entire thing up like I've done in the past."

"Are you talking about golf now?"

Janet eyed her partner. "Yes, I'm talking about this stupid game! Now let me hit."

Janet yanked the driver out of her bag and grabbed her tee from her pocket. She kneeled and stuck the tee firmly into the ground. She didn't want to break this one. She only thought to bring one tee since she didn't think she would have lasted this long playing the game.

"I don't have as much strength as you, but I will hit it with precision as hard as I can," Janet said without looking at her partner. "You always did make fun of my lack of strength."

"I don't think I made fun of it. I simply said you weren't as strong as I am, so you wouldn't be so hard on yourself."

"That's your point of view. Now let me hit," Janet said. She squared her club head to the ball and adjusted her stance. She wanted to hit it hard to prove herself, but she knew it may compromise her accuracy. She swung the club, and it landed behind her left shoulder.

"Wow! That one flew!" her partner said.

"Dang it! I hooked it over the trees. It's not on the fairway!"

"Yes, but maybe it made it to the green. You said it went left of the fairway."

"I just wanted to make it to the middle of the fairway. Then I could have an easy shot to the green. We will never find the ball."

"Don't lose hope. Remember the angels are on our side."

Janet pursed her lips and grabbed her cart. "Okay. Get your flashlight out. It's probably in someone's fenced backyard, but we will check. If we don't find it, I'm done playing this game."

## Hole 4

Day delayed its radiant rays. The sun should have been tipping over the horizon by now, but angels may have barricaded the light with their shields to continue the night game.

"I can't believe my ball fell just at the outer corner of the sand trap near the green. If I didn't hit it so hard, I could have gotten another birdie, but par is still amazing. I believe this is beginning to be my best game ever. Though, we still have six holes left.

I'm on a roll, but I could still falter and lose my game," Janet said.

"I don't want you to lose your game. That's the whole point of why we are here. Before you tee up, tell me something since you are in such a good mood."

"Don't ruin this for me with talk," Janet said.

"Why did you stop playing golf? It's obvious you love it."

Janet could feel the heat rise from her cheeks even though the cool breeze blew across it. "You know exactly why."

"I understand there is a period of processing pain, but you are beyond that point. And, honestly, I've seen you process nothing, which is why you are on prescribed medication. How long do you want to take those pills? If you would deal with what's bothering you, you could be off them. And the alcohol coping."

"I don't get drunk often," Janet said. "Why are you judging me? You used to drink."

"Yes, but I did it in celebration or when we were on a date. I didn't take shots to cope. You may not be getting drunk, but you are coping with something you haven't dealt with."

"What? Are you the therapist now? I thought you were my husband. Are you no longer going to play this game? You have no right to analyze me," Janet said.

"You're right. I'm not a therapist. Your twin is. I'm a pilot."

Janet put her driver back into the bag. "I don't want to talk about your piloting! I'm done playing this game! Take me home."

Her partner held up yielded hands. "Okay, you are right. I pushed. I don't want to analyze you. I think your twin has just been rubbing off on me is all. Please, continue to play."

Janet looked at her golf bag. "Fine, but only because I am playing well. Maybe the angels *are* on my side." She walked to the tee box and placed her only tee into the ground. "This one is the longest hole on the front nine. I'm going to try to hit it even harder. There is only one sand trap, but the green is a steep hill around it. If my ball can make it halfway down the fairway, I may have a chance."

Janet hit the ball. This time she knew she hit with precision. No angels needed on this hole.

"Beautiful shot!" her partner exclaimed.

"Thank you," Janet said, smiling. The smile suddenly caused anxiety to rear up. She hadn't smiled like that in over a year.

"What's wrong?" her partner asked.

"No, it's nothing. I just haven't smiled in a while."

"We know."

"All of you?"

"Mom, your kids, your twin—yes, they all haven't seen you smile since that day."

Janet's heart began to squeeze in her chest. Another anxiety attack would hit her soon if she didn't distract herself. "Let's go find my ball. I know right where it is."

"Are you alright?"

"No, and I forgot to bring my pills. We may have to cut this game short."

"Let us see this smile not as a bad thing. Let us see it as a good thing."

"I don't deserve to smile," Janet said.

"What does that mean? Of course, you do."

Janet didn't answer as the pair walked down the fairway. Janet throttled her golf pushcart, and it fell.

"I hate this thing. I miss the days when we would drive a golf cart," she said, kicking the fallen bag.

"Here, let me push it for a while," her partner said, picking up the pushcart and bag.

Janet looked away and quickly wiped the tears that had fallen down her cheeks. She thought her days of crying were over. This game was opening wounds she wanted to be left alone.

"There I see your ball!" her partner exclaimed. "It's right in front of the hill to the green."

The tears instantly stopped. She had never hit the ball so far. She would have to use her pitching wedge. She never liked using it, but at least the ball was on the grass and not in the sand. When they arrived, she searched through her golf bag. "Dang it! I forgot my pitching wedge!"

"What does that mean?"

"It means I won't be able to make it up that hill without it. I will not get par on this hole. The angels are gone."

"Here," her partner said bringing out an iron. "Just use this one."

"A seven? That won't help."

"Just try it. You might get it up the hill."

Janet grabbed the iron. She wanted to get this game over with. It was nice when she was doing well, but not having the correct club irritated her husband. She looked at her partner. "Normally, you would be angry with me if I forgot my club. Now it's like you don't even care about the game."

"I do care. I just have faith you can make it with this club. Everything happens for a reason."

"I never liked using the wedge anyway," Janet said and squared the iron face to the ball and moved her feet to follow suit. She swung and the golf ball lifted into the air and soared into the green dropping right in front of the hole.

"Did it go in?" Janet asked excitedly.

"I don't know! I couldn't see it once it started rolling."

Janet ran up the hill to the fourth hole. "I can't believe it! I got an eagle! I have never ever gotten an eagle!"

Her partner came up beside her with the golf pushcart. "If memory serves me, I think I did once."

"Yes, you did," Janet nodded. "You would be so proud of me."

"I am proud of you," her partner said.

Janet removed the flag and retrieved her ball. "Thank you." She couldn't help smiling again. This time it didn't feel so bad.

## Hole 5

Everything remained still on the golf course except the cars on the street beyond the grass began to drive the streets with their headlights beaming. A few ducks and other waterfowl splashed in the man-made lakes adorning the greens, but their whistling songs were calming and natural. Janet watched as her partner dragged her golf pushcart behind her.

"You know you don't have to drag it behind you," she said.

"This feels better. Dragging it on the grass is easier than pushing it through the grass."

"You always did things differently. Ever since we were young."

"Well, we met at sixteen. You should know my ways by now."

Janet looked away. "That's right. We did meet at a young age. Maybe too early. We became more like siblings."

"Why is that?" her partner asked.

"You know how it was. We were so busy living our own lives. Once the kids left the house, we had nothing to bring us together. You had your piloting jobs, and I had my literary agency," Janet said. "You wanted to retire, but I didn't want to. Our house was paid off. We had plenty of retirement saved up. You wanted to travel the world."

"We can't hold onto regrets like that, and we still had our golf game together," her partner said.

"Yes, golf was the one thing a week we did together. Then lunch and drinks. You always wanted to play eighteen holes, but I wouldn't."

"I just like the game so much."

Janet shook her head. "It was more than that. I think you wanted to spend more time with me. You complained I was constantly going to writers' conferences, but I needed to attend them to find more authors."

"You have an impressive list of writers already. They make you a lot of money. Most of them continue to write multiple books."

"I don't know. I think I liked the prestige of it. Men and women trying to impress me so badly. They would offer me their first-class seats on the plane. But I really didn't need to go to those conferences. I had writers contacting my assistant constantly through my website. You wanted me to stay home more often, but I had my conferences that I went to every year. I wouldn't miss them. They made me feel good."

"And I didn't make you feel good?"

Janet said nothing.

"Maybe I should have gone with you," her partner said.

"You suggested it, but I said you would have been bored. A pilot surrounded by a bunch of creatives."

"I could have done my own thing during the day. Walked the city. Gone hiking. Checked out the local restaurants. We could have done stuff at night."

"No, the conferences have day classes and night meetings. There would have been no room for your presence."

"Oh," her partner said.

"We are here. You can set the bag down. This is a short fairway but difficult. Lots of sand traps and trees. I usually hit it a fourth of the way from the green. Sometimes I make par. Other times I bogey. It's the oak trees that will get you."

"Here," her partner said. "Your driver."

Janet took the driver. "Thank you." Then she reached in her pocket for the tee. "Oh no! I left the tee at the last hole!"

"Don't you worry. I have plenty," her partner said, pulling out half a dozen tees from a pant pocket.

"How do you have tees?"

"I told you. I've been planning this outing for a while. You just weren't listening."

Janet took one of the tees. "No, I just didn't care."

"I see light starting to appear," her partner said, looking at the horizon. "Do we need to hurry? Will they get mad?"

"The greenspeople won't say anything. They know me. They probably think I'm still a member. But the golf pro or general manager may say something, but they won't be here for another hour or so. We have time. I usually get par on this hole, but I could still mess it up," Janet said.

"Think positively," her partner said.

"I haven't thought positively in over a year," Janet answered.

"I know. You are rewiring your brain with negative thoughts. It's not good and it is starting to show. That is why I am here with you. You can't get rid of what you won't acknowledge. It will only get worse. Your negative thought patterns will eventually completely rearrange your mind into something ugly."

"I think it is too late for that," Janet said. She put the new tee in the ground. "I will hit it toward the green. Then I will get it onto the green. Finally, I will get it in the hole. That will be par for this hole." As she swung, she sensed what felt like an embrace on her arms and waist. Like someone was behind her, swinging with her.

"Hole in one! Hole in one!" her partner screamed.

"What?" Janet asked, confused. "That can't be possible. I've never gotten a hole in one. I'm not a professional golfer. I'm an amateur."

"An amateur who just got a hole in one!" her partner said, laughing. "Wow! This game is fun."

Janet stood stunned. She didn't know if her husband would be proud or jealous. He had never gotten a hole in one.

"I felt something," Janet began.

Her partner turned toward her. "What did you feel? Joy? Freedom? Relief?"

She shook her head. "No, not a feeling. I felt an embrace while I teed off. It was only a whisper of a feeling, but it definitely wasn't the wind. It was like the embrace was guiding my shot."

"I'm telling you. There are angels with us today." Her partner gave a knowing smile.

"You and your angels," Janet said. "Let's hurry to hole six. I see the sun tipping over the horizon."

## Hole 6

Feelings of dread again squeezed at Janet's chest. She wished she had brought her pills or at least a flask of something to drink. The golf course was bringing back too many bad memories. "This is the hole you never liked. I forgot about it. You threw your iron into the water one day."

"Did I always get upset?" her partner asked.

"No, just sometimes I think I was the one who made you upset, and the bad shot just put you over the edge."

"Why is that?"

Janet shrugged. "I guess I complained a lot."

"What do you mean?"

Janet looked at her partner. "I'm sure you know."

"I know a little but tell me more."

"I'd say you were driving the golf cart too fast, or you turned too fast. I'd get on you for using the restroom every time we passed one. If another set of golfers were coming up behind us, I would make us skip a hole to get further up—even your favorite ones. I was embarrassed and didn't want them to have to wait on us. I remember even once getting on you for your wind-blown hair. Now that I look back on it, I wonder why you wanted to golf with me. I wasn't very fun unless I was doing well. And if you were doing well and I wasn't, I was jealous and would start nitpicking more."

"I'm surprised by your honesty," her partner said.

"Isn't that why we are here? You want my honesty? Can we leave now? All this honesty is ruining my excitement of my well-played game."

"But what about your hole in one you just got? You said yourself that you've never played this well. We need to finish playing this game. It may change your life."

"Golf won't change anything," Janet said.

"Yes, but this game may? Here, take your driver. Tell me about this hole."

Janet took the driver and brought the tee out of her pocket. "It's nothing spectacular, but it was one of your favorites besides hole nine because this one is the second longest fairway and has a creek on the right of the green. Hole nine is next to the country club. You loved showing off in front of the other golfers."

"Maybe I just wanted to be appreciated for my skill. We played for twenty-four years almost every week."

Janet put the tee in the ground. "You wanted the attention. I wasn't very good at complimenting you. I guess I didn't think you needed it. You were always so jovial. Why did I need to add more to it?"

"Yes, but I'm your husband. I need to hear nice words from my wife. Didn't you like hearing nice words from your authors?"

Janet stood and readied her driver. "I did because you stopped giving me nice words."

"Why do you think I stopped giving them?" her partner asked.

"Probably because I never gave them to you. Why should I? You always had a cheerful attitude. I needed to hear them more."

"You know a cheerful attitude is a choice, as is a sour one."

Janet held her tears back. The sun was rising, and she didn't want to be seen crying. "Then the kids left the house one by one and there were no more words left. All I had were want-to-be writers who flattered me because they wanted a contract." She looked away. "Just let me hit this ball."

Right when she hit the ball, she knew she sliced it. The ball soared right and continued to roll toward the creek. Suddenly, a large swan got out of the water and pecked at her ball while it was rolling. He stopped it from going in the water.

"You see! Angels!" her partner said. "You're near the green!"

"I've never seen that happen," Janet said, as she watched the swan go back into the water.

"Can you play the ball?"

"Yes, if an animal touches your ball while it is in motion, you play it where it lies. That ball would have been at the bottom of the creek now if the swan hadn't stopped it."

"How many shots do you have to make par?"

"Two more. I will have to hit it into the green and then into the hole."

"You haven't had a bogey yet!" her partner said.

"I know," Janet said, putting the driver back into the bag. "I would have usually bogeyed by now. Let's hurry. I see the greenspeople here."

They made their way to the ball near the creek. "It's another steep incline. I wish I had my wedge." She looked through her bag. "Wait a minute." She grabbed a club. "My wedge is right here. How did I not see it before?"

"Maybe it's God's way of telling you that you don't have to have everything perfect. It's okay sometimes to not do what's expected of you."

"Well, I'm playing this game, aren't I? That is out of the norm for me."

Her partner smiled. "I'm glad you are. I think our time here is helping."

Janet aimed the head of her wedge next to the ball and adjusted her feet. "Maybe," was all she said before she hit the ball.

## Hole 7

Getting to the seventh hole was difficult without a golf cart. The course turned and the walk was long. Janet looked at the sky. The sun was almost completely above the horizon now. The country club staff would be here soon.

"Maybe we should finish up here. I don't want us to get in trouble."

"What's the worst they can do? Tell us to leave. No, I want to do my favorite one at hole nine. You said hole seven is short. Then we will just have two left. I want to see you have a perfect game."

"Hole seven is short but the walk to it takes time. Do you want me to push my clubs now?" Janet asked.

"No, I kind of like doing it. I appreciate it when you let me help you. Sometimes you can be stubborn. You don't accept help enough. There are people who care about you and want to support you. Your mom, your kids and your twin sister all want to help you."

Janet walked and looked around the golf course. She did miss this place. The air was cool, but the sun was finally out. The birds sang their songs and the grass radiated greener than she remembered. Even the air smelled organic. Maybe she would renew her membership, but she would have to pay the twenty-thousand-dollar membership fee again. Didn't matter though. She had plenty of money. Too much money. Money she wished she never had received.

"What are you thinking?" her partner asked.

"I hate to admit it, but I kind of miss this place. But wouldn't it be weird coming back after the accident? I would hate for people to pity me."

"They may for a while, but after a few months, things would go back to normal."

"A new normal," Janet said. "I don't know if I like a new normal."

"Honey, that's life," her partner said. "Things happen, and we adjust. I see you every time you hit your ball, you adjust your feet. The ball is in a new place, and you have to compensate. That's life. Sometimes our ball is in a new place, and we must adjust."

"And that's why we are here. You want me to adjust."

Her partner stopped pulling the cart. "Yes, but you can't adjust unless you know where your ball is."

"I lost my ball," Janet said. Now tears wetted her cheeks. She didn't bother wiping them away.

"Let God be your ball for now. I don't know what the future holds, but He may give you a new ball."

"Why would He give me a new ball when I discarded the one I had?"

"What do you mean?" her partner asked.

Janet finally wiped her tears. "We are here. Just let me hit this ball. I don't want to think about these things."

"That's exactly my point. You can't adjust your feet if you don't think about these things."

"Hand me my driver," Janet said roughly.

"Here," her partner said. "What is the par on this one?"

"Three, but you always got a birdie here. I simply got par, which is adequate." She pushed the tee into the ground. This time she wouldn't let emotions mess with her game. There was no creek and no swan to stop her ball from getting lost. She adjusted her feet once more and swung leading with her hips. Right when the club face hit the ball, she knew the shot was good. It was a short course, and her ball landed on the green about three club lengths away from the hole.

"Oh my gosh! You might get a birdie!" her partner exclaimed.

"That's how you always did it. I'm simply copying you. I just need my putter. Follow me, and let's hurry to hole eight, so we can finish this game."

The pair walked to the green. The ball was even closer than Janet had anticipated. It was about two and a half club lengths from the hole. She stared at the green for several seconds.

"What are you analyzing?" her partner asked.

"I'm looking at the slope of the grass. I'm seeing if the dew on the grass has dried up. I'm looking for debris. And I'm making sure no squirrel or any other animal will touch my ball and ruin my shot."

"That swan sure did help," her partner said.

"That's different. The ball was still moving. I can make this shot. I don't want an animal moving it."

Her partner looked around. "No squirrel or bird in sight. Make the shot and you'll get another birdie."

Janet moved the line of her ball to face the hole. She always used the line marking the ball. It helped her gauge where to put her feet. "It's downhill, so I need to tap the ball just barely. Grass is fairly dry. The slope moves slightly to the right, so I will aim left-center of the hole. "

"Have you ever gotten a birdie on this hole?" her partner asked.

"Yes, and you were thrilled. You forced me to have a glass of port after lunch to celebrate. Port is so sweet, but I drank it only because you bragged about me to our waitress."

"Then let's see it again! Then we can celebrate with a glass of port."

"I thought you stopped drinking?"

"Well, I will drink a glass of port to celebrate you!"

Janet looked at her partner and could see the image of her husband's face in the sunlight. "That would be nice," she said as tears streamed down her face. "I would have a glass of port with you every day and never bicker again."

"Is that what this is about? Your treatment of me?"

Janet wiped the tears away. "I see Brad, the golf pro, parking his car. Let me make this birdie and we can hide behind the bathroom of the seventh hole until he goes into the country club. He does paperwork for about thirty minutes to an hour before he starts his lessons."

## Hole 8

He finally walked into the club house after talking with the greenspeople for several minutes. The golf pro normally didn't chat with the greenspeople for long. She wondered if the country club was planning on changes to the golf course. Lord knows it was old and needed to be updated. That was the only reason she could play well in the dark. She played the same holes for so many years.

"Okay, we can head to the eighth hole," she said. She knew they didn't have much time, but now she actually wanted to finish this game. Something was welling up inside of her, and she wanted to know what it was. Maybe it would help her stop the downward spiral she was on. Her drinking. Her pills. Barely making her work obligations. She felt like she was on the verge of drowning, always gasping for air and never ahead of the game. If something didn't happen, her mom, her kids or her twin would admit her to a hospital. She had hidden her condition well for almost a year, but it was getting worse.

"This one is not long, but it twists and there are many trees and several sand traps. This one is par three, but you always got a birdie. I never made par on this one. My ball landed in the sand trap almost every time."

"Then maybe you should do something different," her partner said.

"You know, you would suggest that, and I would ignore your words. Now I think I'll take your advice. Give me my smaller driver, the hybrid. You bought it for me, and I said I absolutely hated it. But now I think it will be perfect for this shot."

"Which one is the hybrid?" her partner asked.

"You want to play this game with me, but you can't even remember what you bought me?"

"It was a long time ago. I remember you telling me you hated it," her partner said.

Janet snatched the hybrid club from the bag. "It's nice to know you were listening. Makes me wonder if you are listening now."

"I'm here, aren't I? I'm listening to every word you're saying, but you aren't saying enough!"

"Don't get rude with me. This was all your idea. It doesn't matter, though. I will finish these nine holes for my benefit."

"Good, glad to hear you say that because I'm tired of pushing you."

"Whatever," Janet said simply. She knew she sounded like a child, but she didn't care. She needed to finish this game. If only to get people off her back.

She carefully placed the tee in the ground in a spot she normally wouldn't. "I always veer too far to the right because the course goes right. I'd overcompensate. Let's try hitting it straight with a slight angle in my stance." She did two practice swings just to get the rhythm of the hybrid club she never used. Then she thrust her hips toward the flag and her taut arms swung up and behind her. The ball sailed straight and slightly right. It soared over the trees to where the flag was visible.

"If I'm not mistaken, I bet my ball landed just by the green!"

"Let's go find out!" her partner said, running and dragging the golf bag pushcart from behind.

Janet couldn't help but laugh. She ran after her partner with her hybrid club still in her hand. When they rounded the trees, they could see the ball just near the green.

"I can't believe it! I might actually make par on the eighth hole. I've never made par before!"

"What do you need? Your wedge?"

Janet shook her head. "No, give me the seven iron again. Maybe doing things the non-perfect way is helping me."

"I still think the angels are guiding you," her partner said.

Janet remembered the brief embrace when she made that amazing hole in one shot on hole five. "Maybe you are right. Maybe God is trying to tell me something."

"I think He's been trying to tell you something for over a year."

Janet felt the tears sting her eyes again. "I know. I need to forgive."

"Forgive who? Janet, who do you need to forgive? Nothing was your fault!"

Janet again wiped the tears on the back of her black sleeve. "Let me just make these two shots. I will hit it to the hole and then hit it in. Then we can finish hole nine."

"My favorite hole?" her partner asked.

Janet nodded and swung the iron, and the ball dropped inches away from the hole.

"I can't believe it," Janet said. "I'm going to make par."

She grabbed her putter and walked to the ball lying next to the hole and easily putted it in. "I did it!"

"I am so proud of you," her partner said.

Janet began to weep. Her partner took hold of her shoulders. "I will always be proud of you."

"No, you wouldn't. Not if you knew what I did."

"What did you do?"

"I'm too ashamed to say," Janet faltered. "Let me finish the ninth hole. That was your favorite and you always wanted to get a birdy to show off, but you never did."

"Then let's finish this game," her partner said. They began to walk to the ninth hole. Staff were walking the grounds, but none of them seem to notice them. The sun was fully in the sky and the grass smooth and dry under their shoes.

# Hole 9

If *I could just make this last hole a birdie,* Janet thought, *then I could be redeemed. Maybe my husband has forgiven me.*

"What are you thinking?" her partner asked.

Janet's head dropped. "I was a terrible wife. I took my husband for granted, and now he's gone."

"So, we are no longer role-playing?" her twin asked.

Janet stared at her twin's face. "No, thank you, though, for getting me out here and pretending to be my husband. I know I've been terrible to you and Mom. I'm dying inside because I lost him. The lightning hit his plane. There was nothing he could do. They all died, and my last words to him before he left were awful. He wanted to retire. He wanted me to retire. He wanted to travel the world, but I wouldn't. My identity was so wrapped up in my kids, and when they left, I wrapped it up in work. Why couldn't I have wrapped my life around my husband."

"That is why you wrap your life around God. When we love God most, we love others even more."

Janet covered her face with her hands and began to cry. The greenspeople noticed them now. "Can God ever forgive me. He gave me a husband who was so good to me. We were married for twenty-four years, and I just became a sour, bitter wife. He was always in a good mood despite my irritableness. He wanted to spend time with me. Go on vacations with me. And what did I do? I'd yelled at him for leaving his shoes out. I'd patronize him every time he made even a little mistake. I shunned his sexual advances, and when we did make love, I endured it like I was doing him a favor. This man who truly loved me—adored me—is gone, and I can't tell him that I'm so sorry. I wish I could redo our entire marriage, but it is too late."

"I'm so sorry, Janet. I knew you were struggling, and I figured that was the reason."

Janet looked at her twin. "You would tell me. You would say if I didn't treat him right and respect him, there would be a line of women wanting him. I didn't listen. He never cheated on me, but his life cheated on me. Stole him before I could understand what I was losing. Now all I have is regret. I can't live a life of regret. It's killing me. I got two million dollars from his life insurance, but I would give it all back to have him again."

Janet's twin took her into her arms. "I know he was a Christian. He loved the Lord. He's in Heaven, and I'm sure he wouldn't want you living like this. He adored you. He would want your suffering to end. If you can't forgive yourself for your own well-being, do it for his."

Janet didn't bother wiping her tears. "Okay, if that is true then let me get a birdie on the ninth hole, and I will forgive myself for being a terrible wife."

Janet's twin smiled. "The angels have been helping us the entire time. Don't think they will stop now."

Janet picked the driver out of the bag. Many of the country club workers were watching her. She also recognized several members she had been friends with before her husband's death. She placed the ball on the tee and hit mid-strength. The fairway wasn't long. The ball landed to the right of the green near where the people were watching her.

"What is the par on this one?" her twin asked.

"It's par three again. There are more par fours on the back nine. They really need to update the course." She looked back to where her ball landed. "I will have to make it in the hole in the next shot to make a birdie. If I do, I will forgive myself. If I don't, I deserve to suffer."

"You will make it. I know you will."

Janet began walking toward her ball. She could hear her sister praying under her breath next to her.

When she got to the ball, there was a crowd of people watching her. Her ball was inches from the green. To make this shot would be a miracle. She ignored the voices behind her. Her twin sister came up beside her and handed her the putter.

"I demand that ball to go into the hole in Jesus' name," she shouted.

Janet lined up the ball. The surface of the green was fairly flat. She needed only to hit the ball straight. She placed the face of the club head against the ball and altered her stance to follow suit. The sun was bright now and the cool weather had warmed. She would have taken off her jacket, but the moment of truth was now. She inhaled slowly and straightened her shoulders. No torso in this move. Just shoulder and arm movement. She tapped the ball, and it rolled onto the green, straight to the hole.

Instead of her heart tensing, it began to pump with excitement. The ball looked like it would go in. Gasps from the onlookers could be heard. The ball moved to the hole and stopped just at the lip of the hole.

"Oh no!" her twin cried.

Suddenly, Janet saw something. A figure by her ball. It brushed her ball into the hole and disappeared. The crowd behind them cheered. She had made a birdie on the ninth hole. Her husband had forgiven her.

"You did it! You did it!" her twin yelled, jumping up and down with excitement.

"Did you see it?" Janet asked, looking at her twin.

"See what?"

"There was a figure. It brushed the ball into the hole."

Her twin smiled. "You see. I told you angels were with us."

Janet smiled and hugged her sister. "I forgive myself for being a terrible wife. Thank you for playing this game with me. I'm ready to move on."

"I can't believe you got a birdie on the ninth hole, Janet," a voice said from behind her.

It was Brad the golf pro. "Sorry I'm golfing since I'm not a member anymore. My sister was doing some therapy on me."

"You know, we want you back at the club. We know what you have been through, and your loss has been great. The board members and I agreed that if you ever wanted your membership back, we would waive the membership fee of the twenty thousand."

Janet felt a calmness pour over her like warm oil. "Yes, I would like that very much. I would like to golf again. I'm retiring, so I will be around the club a lot more. Maybe I will even join the board since you have been asking me for years."

Brad smiled. "We would like that."

"Maybe I should join," Janet's sister interjected. "I really enjoyed watching Janet play."

"Heck, I'm sure the board will waive your membership fee as well since you got us one of our favorite members back."

Janet laughed and looked at her twin. "You have a lot to learn, but I'll catch you up. That's the least I can do for what you have done for me. Now let me get my ball."

Janet walked to the flag waving from the hole where she just achieved a birdie. As she reached for the ball, she noticed a single silvery white feather. *I guess God's into cheating too,* she mused. *He cheated for me, and I'll take that cheat gladly.*

# Devotional Study

I don't know why I chose the name "Janet." It just came to me. I knew that my main character's name must be Janet. When I finished writing this longish short story, I looked up her name, and I was surprised by what I found. The name Janet means "God is gracious" or "gift from God." How fitting. God was gracious to Janet that day to send her twin sister and His angels to help her. I do have an identical twin sister who is a therapist. She helped me through an extremely difficult season in my life that prophetic people usually go through. Every prophet I have read has gone through a time of intense spiritual warfare. That time made me stronger, but I never want to go through it again. I felt like a prisoner of war in my own mind for two years, which is not a great thing for an introvert. Although I didn't feel it at the time, I know Jesus was with me every second of every day.

The main theme of this short story is taking our spouses for granted. I see it all the time. Husbands and wives taking each other for granted and allowing their love for each other to grow cold. It truly is sad when we start focusing on our spouse's weaknesses and not their strengths. I used to get upset about constantly picking up my husband's shoes. I would think in Heaven he would see the pile of shoes I picked up for him during our marriage. But then God whispered something to me. He said, "Daniel does things for you that you don't notice or appreciate." Now when I pick up his shoes, I have faith and appreciation for whatever it is he's doing for me that I can't see. Though, there is a feather in this story, it is mostly symbolic. I don't necessarily believe angels have wings, but they do fly, and they are out here helping us. But I thought having the silvery-white feather on the ninth hole would be symbolic that God truly did send His angels to help Janet. God loves Janet. He wants her to heal. And her twin sister loves her too.

> *"Above all, have fervent and unfailing love for one another, because love covers a multitude of sins [it overlooks unkindness and unselfishly seeks the best for others]"* (1 Peter 4:8 AMP).

## Reflection Questions

Have you ever taken your spouse or a loved one for granted? How did it affect your relationship and your viewpoint of that person? Is there something you can do to fan the flames of love? Can you aggressively make choices and actions that will lead to a more enjoyable and loving relationship?

# Five Literary Devices

1. **Hyperbole:** An exaggeration used for emphasis.

**Short Story:** "If I hit a house, I will poison your water and dump your body in the Gulf of Mexico."

**Bible:** *"If your right eye causes you to stumble, gouge it out and throw it away. It is better for you to lose one part of your body than for your whole body to be thrown into hell. And if your right hand causes you to stumble, cut it off and throw it away. It is better for you to lose one part of your body than for your whole body to go into hell"* (Matthew 5:29-30 NIV). Jesus told us He fulfilled the Mosaic Law on our behalf, and he left us with one final command: Love God, love others, love yourself (Mark 12:30-31), so His words here are emphasizing the need to control our eyes and hands. He is not being literal; rather, he is using a literary device as emphasis.

2. **Merism: A list of opposing ideas that together** make a complete whole.

**Short Story:** "An atmosphere of stillness saturated the golf course, yet the tension between the two golf partners overshadowed the calm. The stillness and the tension formed the totality of life—both the good and the bad."

**Bible:** *"You will not fear the terror of night, nor the arrow that flies by day, nor the pestilence that stalks in the darkness, nor the plague that destroys at midday"* (Psalm 91:5-6 NIV).

3. **Numerology:** Numbers being used in a symbolic way.

**Short Story:** I ended the story on the ninth hole not simply because it's half the course, but because the number nine biblically represents divine completeness. Christ died on the ninth hour of the day. I wanted to convey that Janet finally received divine completion in her healing on the ninth hole.

**Bible:** Numbers have great meaning in the Bible. Seven is one of the most powerful because it represents the day of Sabbath that God rested and Christ did His work of saving the world and redeeming all of us back to God (Matthew 12:8).

4. **Rhetorical Question:** A question asked without expecting an answer.

**Short Story:** "What? Are you the therapist now? I thought you were my husband. Are you no longer going to play this game?"

**Bible:** "What shall we say about such wonderful things as these? If God is for us, who can ever be against us?" (Romans 8:31 NLT).

5. **Wordplay:** Making a play on word meanings.

**Short Story:** "Are you talking about the golf now?' Janet eyed her partner. 'Yes, I'm talking about this stupid game! Now let me hit.'" I do a wordplay here of the word "game." They are playing the game of golf, but they are also playing the game of roleplay. Janet's twin is roleplaying as her husband to give her closure from his death.

**Bible:** *"I am your servant Ruth,' she said. 'Spread the corner of your garment over me, since you are a guardian-redeemer of our family'"* (Ruth 3:9 NIV). Ruth in this scene uncovers Boaz's feet and says this phrase of covering her, which represents marriage. She is in essence asking Boaz to marry her. Her boldness is why Ruth is one of my favorite women in the Bible and is my daughter's middle name.

## Bonus Device

- **Acrostic:** I wrote each hole with the first letter of each sentence in consecutive order with our alphabet, so A, B, C, D, E, F, G, H and I. Nine letters and nine holes. The Bible does this (Psalm 119), but it can only be seen in the original language of Hebrew. This goal helped me not to start with dialogue, which I tend to do, and this story is almost all dialogue. I wanted the first symbol to be a letter, not an open quote mark. It caused me to be more creative at detailing the setting of the story.

# HEAVENLY STREET WALK

I opened my eyes surprised that the bright light surrounding me didn't cause my eyelids to squint. I looked down at my hands. My aged, arthritic fingers shone with youth and wellness—no longer contorted from years of typing. The pain radiating over my body as I lie in the hospice bed waiting for God to take me home vanished. All I could do was pray during those final lingering months. I remember the moans of my children and grandchildren, but the forlorn atmosphere suddenly lifted, replaced by something to be giddy about.

"Thank God I'm finally dead," I whispered, laughing to myself. My life had been one of blessed struggles. God gave me everything I never thought to ask for—an amazing husband and children, wealth, beauty, and health until old age caught up with me. However, the promise He had given me in my youth did not come to be. My faith never faltered; though, discouragement of the weight of "hope deferred" had become a thorn in my side. I continued to write books—more than a hundred of them—for His glory, but the readers never came. For almost fifty years I wrote in the private corners of my life with no fruit to show for it. My husband spent our money gladly to support my book babies who always died at birth. Every book I wrote wrecked me with anxiety, and every one I published drowned me in depression because I knew few readers would hold the blessed cover in their hands.

"Thank God that is over. At least I stayed the course. I might not have anything to show for my life, but I didn't veer to the left or the right. God told me to write regardless of the outcome. People thought I was crazy, but what could I do? The outcome was in His hands. I only had to be obedient," I reiterated to myself like I had done for years on Earth. "But no more of that!"

My smile widened. The struggle to gain God's promise that I would reach millions for Christ with my writing was over. I was finally dead on Earth and in my true home. During my time of writing, I had gone from striving to an emotional breakdown, to a two-year spiral of spiritual attacks, another two years of coping and, finally, to the realization that I only needed to obediently write. I couldn't force God's hand, and I chose to love Him despite knowing that He gave me a promise that I would never see fulfilled. My life might have nothing to show for all the hard work I did, but I grew into the image of Christ. Maybe that was all my writing was meant to accomplish—for me to mature and to become the best version of myself before I entered eternity.

"Doesn't matter now," I said. "I am young. I am home. And I feel so much joy to be here. I hope my family doesn't mourn for me too much. If they knew the majesty and ecstasy of this place, they would rejoice in my departure."

I set my eyes before me. It was time to explore my permanent home and go find Jesus. If He could just wrap me in His arms, the complete peace that seemed to elude me in the land of the living would finally be mine. I knew I would at least get a smallish "well done good and faithful servant." I might not have achieved His promise for me, but I had been a wonderful wife, a tremendous mother and a servant of others. I shared the Gospel with those who would listen, and all my books brimmed with the Good News of Jesus Christ—both my nonfiction and fiction alike. They were still down on earth unopened and unread, but I wrote my God-given stories to the best of my imperfect ability.

"Now, let me go find my Lord!" I exclaimed leaping into my first step. The feeling of youth flooded my new body, and I couldn't help but take several more leaps on the shiny glass-like golden road that led toward a mountain covered in a rainbow of colored flowers—many colors I had never beheld and could not describe even if I knew all the languages of Earth. The fragrant aroma of the flowers filled my nostrils even though I was yet a distance away. Such a variety of scents all at once would have given me a headache on Earth, but now they mingled into a pleasing, dramatic aroma. The gold street felt silken under my energetic bare feet. I looked down and knelt. I could see my pretty, young reflection. The wrinkles, age spots and sags were gone. "I'm even prettier now than I was in my youth." I glided my fingers along the glossy road. Though it looked like golden glass, it felt like the smooth surface of a still spring of water.

Suddenly, I heard a beautiful roar and looked up. Hundreds or even thousands of angelic beings, more beautiful than any priceless paintings adorning the walls of countless museums, surrounded the shimmering blue sky around the mountain. Their voices vibrated with shouts of glory, and the praise made my heart pound with expectation. Even the mountain and the flowers appeared to be crying out the glory of the Lord. My feet walked toward the powerfully awe-inspiring noise. I knew that Jesus' throne haloed with a rainbow would be just in front of the mountain. Then I would finally bow at his feet, and hopefully He would lift me into a long-anticipated embrace.

As I continued to walk, a massive angel unexpectedly appeared before me and blocked my view. I was not scared but slightly startled.

"Hello, honored one," he said plainly.

I wanted to laugh, but I knew what happened to Sarah when she laughed about becoming pregnant in her old age. Her lack of faith becoming apparent. "Hello," I said. "I don't know why, but I have a feeling you are Michael, the Archangel."

He nodded knowingly. "Your husband saw me and Gabriel at your house that day."

"Yes, I remember," I said. "That was the day I wanted to die. Demons preyed on my deep discouragement and attacked day and night. I couldn't understand why they would bother with me. I had no platform. I wasn't reaching people for Christ with my writing. My woman's Bible study fell apart. Why did they demonize me so intensely?"

"They knew what you couldn't see," he replied.

"I certainly grew stronger from that time, and I eventually thanked God for it but told Him fervently that I never wanted to be a prisoner of war in my own mind again."

"Here, I have something for you," Michael said. He handed me an intricate sword that reminded me of an Elven sword from the *Lord of the Rings.* The jewel-lined hilt sparkled like a crystal reflecting a multi-colored brilliance of light.

"Warriors are given swords, and this sword is very special. Few people in eternity carry it."

I wanted to tell him he was wrong. I was not a warrior. I had tried to be for twenty years but then succumbed to mere obedience after my breakdown. However, I didn't correct Michael. I knew what happened to Zachariah when he questioned Gabriel, and I didn't want my tongue to be bound up and made mute. I wanted to talk to Jesus face-to-face, not simply by faith. I had talked to Him once in a dream, and the dream became my most favorite.

"Don't worry," Michael laughed, inferring my thoughts. "I'm not going to bind up your tongue. That's Gabriel's trick. If you don't believe that sword is yours, look at the inscription on the hilt on the other side of the jewels."

I held up the sword and turned the hilt until the most elegant handwriting appeared, and my name was written on it. "This is truly my sword?"

He nodded. "Jesus wrote your name on it Himself. Now I had best go. Gabriel needs some help on Earth. Satan and his fallen angels and the trapped ones are in their worst behaviors yet. They know the time is near its end. God's about to do something big."

With that, the Archangel Michael gave me a wink and disappeared.

I gazed at my sword once more, turning it in my hand. It did feel comfortable in my grip like I had owned this sword for a thousand lifetimes. Since I was in eternity now, I had plenty of time to learn to wield it. I continued to walk toward the mountain but noticed that there were now people flanking the golden street. They stared at me and whispered my name. Hundreds and hundreds of people gawked at me like I was a celebrity from Earth. One onlooker walked over to me.

"How did you do it?" he asked.

"Do what?" I asked.

He pointed to my sword. "I've heard rumors about your great exploits on Earth, and that sword is a sign of great faith. Very few people carry it. I personally have never seen the Archangel Michael give one away. You lived an astounding life of faith."

I looked down, ready to feel the embarrassment of shame like I endured every time someone mentioned my books, but still, the joy inside me asserted itself. I could be honest about my failure without humiliation. "No, honestly, my life was completely average. I wrote books, but they rarely sold. I didn't reach many people—though I did work my hardest to. I strove for years and years, doing everything to earn a platform, yet my books never came to life. People of great faith are strong and live in victory. They influence lives and change the world. They have obvious fruit from their efforts of obedience. I too lived in obedience but finally resigned myself to the fact that my life's work would not produce a harvest."

"Oh!" a lady exclaimed. "But it has! I have heard your name being talked about all over the heavenly realm. Your life had a profound effect on

Earth that continues until Jesus returns to His rightful place as King of Kings on Earth as it is in Heaven."

"No," I shook my head. "I was a nobody. I loved and served my family, and I wrote books of faith that never caught on. In fact, every book I wrote cost me more money to write and publish than I received back by many folds. I didn't care about the money, though. I would have written them, published them and given them away freely if they were to transform my readers' lives and free them from Satan's lies. It was ironic really. I wrote about having faith in God's promises, and I never saw my promise realized."

The woman nodded her head with vigor. "No wonder you are a woman of great faith. Your obedience to write those books without seeing the harvest must have been very difficult. Most people would have chased a lesser promise than the promise of the impossible."

"Yes, the books cost me everything and changed no lives. I finally had to tell God I would write for Him even if they never touched a single person. I had to let go of striving and stop trying to force God to keep His promise to me by trying to be perfect."

"Well, I think your point of view from Earth is extremely limited. In Heaven your name is known by many," another man said.

I didn't want to contradict them. They all seemed to genuinely think I made an impact on Earth. "Let me go ask Jesus," I finally said. "He'll be honest about my days on Earth, and I can ask Him why He never fulfilled His promise to me. I'm not angry. Just curious."

As I began to walk down the golden street once more, the people continued to stare at me and whisper. I looked at the sword in my hand and made sure that it was my name written on the hilt. It was.

I continued to walk, and a feeling rose up inside of me. It wasn't pride but more like a sense of accomplishment. I did what the Lord had asked of me, and I knew this truth for certain—I had not been perfect, but I was faithful. I clutched my sword with strength, and my stride morphed with confidence. I ignored the people gathering in a horizontal crowd on either side of the golden road. It didn't matter what they said. I wanted to hear the words of Jesus. Maybe instead of a flat "Well done my good and faithful servant," perhaps I would get the phrase spoken to me more robustly and with enthusiasm.

I saw the first glimmering colors of the rainbow adorning the Lord's throne just as the road went over the horizon. I've seen six-colored rainbows on Earth, but it would take me all of eternity to count the colors in the Lord's rainbow. Then the throne came into view. I abruptly stopped.

The throne appeared to be holographic. When I turned my head one way, I saw an intricately designed throne with ornate details that no craftsman on Earth could create. Yet, when I turned my head another way, I saw a meager manger with cracked wood that was warped with age. I stood there stunned for several seconds, turning my head from left to right.

"It is our Lord," a boy said to me. "I didn't understand it either, but Jesus explained it to me when I first met Him. He said it is the Lamb and the Lion."

Understanding sparked my mind and heart with joy. "Both the Servant and the King," I whispered in agreement.

The boy nodded. Then he looked at my sword. "May I touch it?"

I noticed he held a sword as well but smaller. "I see that you, too, carry a sword."

He held his up with a smile. "My life on Earth was spent mostly in hospital beds. I had leukemia. My parents loved the Lord, and they helped me to love Him too. I stopped questioning why I was sick all the time. And I stopped longing to be someone else. Then I began to enjoy my life even though I knew it would end quickly. I made sure to comfort my parents before I left. They are still on Earth, and I have more brothers and sisters that I can't wait to meet. But I must give them time to earn their swords. I know my mother will have a beautiful one. Maybe even one like yours. She is a praying mother. She prays all the time, and I can hear her prayers here in Heaven. Praying mothers always have beautiful swords."

I presented the sword to the young boy, and he glided his fingers along the jeweled hilt. "I too was a praying mother and from what you told me, I believe she will have her own beautiful sword to carry," I said with confidence.

The boy's smile spread across his gentle face. "I am glad I have met you. Once you meet Jesus, come find me. I would like to have more talks about my family with you, and I would like to hear about yours. From what I have heard, your children are mighty warriors too."

"Yes, I agree. They far surpassed me, which gives me much gladness."

"As it would to any praying mother," he agreed. "Jesus is waiting for you. I just left Him. He is why I knew you were coming. He can't wait to meet you face-to-face."

Then I watched as the boy walked through the crowd carrying his honored sword past the golden road and to the meadows beyond. The people separated for him, allowing him to stroll by. They also whispered his name as they had done mine. My gaze went back to the Lord's throne—humility and power all in one seat. Of course, Jesus would build nothing less as His place of mercy and truth.

I straightened my shoulders in determination and began to jog. The boy had said Jesus was waiting for me, and my anticipation to meet Him overwhelmed me. I began to run faster when I spied a Figure standing in front of the throne. His face shone so brightly that this time I did squint my eyes. But as if the Lord read my mind, He dimmed the bright rays of light, and I could see the Son of Man Who dwelt among us, leaving His throne and taking on flesh. My steps quickened when He reached His arms out wide for me.

"Jesus! Jesus, my Lord!" I cried out. Tears streamed down my face. They were tears of joy that I couldn't stop. I finally slid on my knees and grabbed hold of his ankles, bringing them tightly to my bowed chest. "Jesus! Jesus! Jesus!" was all I could say. My heart welled up with so much love that I could feel nothing else. My promise on Earth meant nothing now. It seemed so small and insignificant compared to the love and joy encapsulating me.

I could hear Jesus' laugh. "Come up, Child. I want to see you."

"But I could stay here a thousand years," I said.

"I know, but stand up. I've been so eager to meet you in Heaven."

I didn't want to move, but a lifetime of obedience caused my legs to rise. I beheld my Savior and all I saw was complete acceptance in His eyes. I grabbed Him into my embrace, and again He laughed a delightful, child-like laugh. He placed His hands on my arms.

"Oh, Child. You were always my deep, sensitive one. You surprised me many times with your resilience and faith. I expanded your influence beyond My original design because you never gave up, and your humility to endure many disappointments and the numerous rejections you received never caused you to deter from the assignment I gave you."

"But how could You be surprised? Don't you know everything?" I asked, releasing my grip around His neck. Again, I beheld His complete acceptance emanating from him. I could show Him all of me—the worst and the best—and He would love me no matter what.

"Didn't the centurion surprise me with his faith?" Jesus asked.

I thought of the Bible story. "Yes," I said. "You said you had not found greater faith in all of Israel."

"I do know all, but I gave you free will. So, knowing does not negate my surprise to the choices you make."

I looked at the ground. "I surprised You?" I asked disbelieving. "I didn't do much of anything great."

He gently tilted my chin back up. "The last will be first, remember? My understanding is beyond the world's comprehension, and you may have not understood My Way fully, but you did obey it. Now let me show you what your faith is doing on Earth."

Then Jesus knelt, and He spread apart the golden floor underneath our feet like sunlight breaking through a cloud. I could see Earth as if through a wide telescope. Outside of time, I could see days, weeks, months and even years laid out instantaneously. What my mind could never comprehend on Earth I could now take in easily.

"I see two groups of people sharing Light fervently," I said. "They are spreading Your love so rapidly. It's more than amazing. I don't have the words. And there is the Archangel Michael hovering above Earth. He is grinning with his arms folded in rest. Now he is nodding to another. It's the Archangel Gabriel! They are both smiling and laughing."

"Yes," the Lord said heartily. "The time has finally come to release my arrows."

I looked to Jesus. "What arrows?"

His eyes focused back to Earth, and I followed his gaze. "You see those two groups of people sharing my love to the nations?"

"Yes," I answered.

"That group," He said pointing to the northwest people, "was ignited by your faith as a mother. Your children and the people you influenced on Earth are now sharing the love you shared with them. They have multiplied exponentially."

I gaped as I watched those people move across the lands spreading light. "Really?"

"Yes," He whispered as if in awe. "And the bigger group of people on the southeast side. Those people are holding and sharing your books—words you wrote to honor Me and share My love."

"No," I said as my hands gripped the edge of the open ground. "That can't be! My books never spread that far and wide! They could never reach that multitude!"

I began to sob as I watched my books float amongst the crowds of people. I knew every cover. I remembered penning every word and publishing every manuscript. Millions of words and tens of thousands of hours I offered to the Lord in my lifetime were now alive and active. They were like my children being carried on the hips of kings and queens, and they shined so brightly that my chest heaved with immense joy. Something lifted from my shoulders, and I felt like a balloon rising. I looked to my Lord. "What did you take off of me?"

"I took off the shackles of *hope deferred* from you—a weight you have grown accustomed to. It was difficult to give you that thorn, but I knew you would accept it because the outcome would be dazzling," He said, nodding to the opening. "Even Michael and Gabriel are amazed, and they don't impress easily."

I stared for a moment longer at my bright books, piercing the hearts of women and men and boys and girls. Then I closed my eyes. "It is finished. I have received my promise," I whispered. Then I stood holding my sword firmly to my side. I looked boldly at my Lord. "The Bible says *hope deferred* is replaced with a *Tree of Life*, and that Tree is You."

Jesus took my hand. "Yes, and now let Me show you the great place I have prepared for you." With His other hand, He handed me a fruit I could not identify. "Here," He said. "Taste the food we have in Heaven. Nothing on Earth compares. Believe me. I ate a variety of foods on Earth when I was there."

I took the fruit and stared. "It is stunning. I find it difficult to eat from such beauty."

He laughed. "Don't worry. You'll get used to the beauty—though, your appreciation of it will never fade."

I brought the fruit to my lips and took a bite of the skin and flesh. My eyes widened. "It is sweet like honey but fragrant like the flowers I smelled on the mountain." I took several more bites as the juices of the fruit ran down my chin. It had been years since I was able to eat fruit without it having to be processed in a blender, so my feeble body could consume it.

"That fragrance is of Heaven. It is in all we eat and drink. It is in the flowers and waters. It is in you too. Now follow me. I have many surprises for you in my Father's house." Then He led me past His rainbowed throne and toward a destination of so much splendor that letters, symbols, paragraphs and stories on Earth could never describe.

## Devotional Study

This is my only published fiction work written in first person and now my second fiction piece based on a dream I had—although much loosely than the first. In first person, the writer is the main character. The writer experiences the story in a personal way when using the pronouns "I" and "me." However, since this story is based on a prophetic dream I had, I thought it only fitting to write in first person and demonstrate my faith in God's promise to me. God gave me a promise, and I will believe it to be true regardless of physical circumstances. My one prayer for others is to have unwavering belief in the promises found in God's Word and the promises the Holy Spirit gives us personally. Jesus asked His disciples if He would find faith on Earth when He returns (Luke 18:8). Our faith is our treasure stored up in Heaven, and it is highly valued by the Lord.

John the Baptist never saw his promise of a Savior realized; though, he preached about it fervently to all who would listen. He was beheaded before Jesus' crucifixion and resurrection, and Jesus noted that John was a man of great faith (Matthew 11:11). John the Baptist preached about a promise he would never personally see fulfilled, and that resolute belief is what Jesus is looking for. The two questions I ask myself: *Will I write my books knowing I may not see their influence in the land of the living and am I willing to toil and sow seeds that I will never see grow and multiply?* That is faith—to believe and work toward the promises of God even when the promises never seem to come true in our time on Earth. God wants our obedience. The outcome is in His hands. My solace, though, is that God knows that "hope deferred makes the heart sick." I don't have to be ashamed when I get discouraged because He understands the effects of hope that is continually deferred. But God also gives a promise that if we can continue to bear the weight of hope, we will eventually gain our ultimate desire: the Tree of Life, Jesus, and all the goodness He has in store for us (Proverbs 13:12).

> *"Now faith is the substance of things hoped for, the evidence of things not seen"* (Hebrews 11:1 KJV).

## Reflection Questions

Have you experienced a season of "Hope Deferred?" Was the weight of hope difficult to bear? Did you wait on the Lord, or did you finally chase a lesser promise? Are you still waiting by faith on a promise the Holy Spirit gave you long ago? How do you encourage yourself and stay expectant of his promise without falling into a pit of discouragement and disbelief?

## Five Literary Devices

1. **Imagery:** Using words to appeal to the reader's five senses: sight, sound, touch, taste and smell.

**Short Story:** In "Heavenly Street Walk" I describe the colors of the flowers (sight) and their aroma (smell). I describe the feel of the golden streets (touch) and the songs of the angelic praises (sound). Finally, I describe the flavors of the heavenly fruit (taste).

**Bible:** *"[I am writing about] what existed from the beginning, what we have heard, what we have seen with our eyes, what we have looked at and touched with our hands, concerning the Word of Life [the One who existed even before the beginning of the world, Christ]—and the Life [an aspect of His being] was manifested, and we have seen [it as eyewitnesses] and testify and declare to you [the Life], the eternal Life who was [already existing] with the Father and was [actually] made visible to us [His followers]—what we have seen and heard we also proclaim to you, so that you too may have fellowship [as partners] with us. And indeed our fellowship [which is a distinguishing mark of born-again believers] is with the Father, and with His Son Jesus Christ. We are writing these things to you so that our joy [in seeing you included] may be* *made complete [by having you share in the joy of salvation]"* (1 John 1:1-4 AMP).

2. **Irony:** A statement or an event that seems contrary to what the reader expects and is often amusing as a result.

**Short Story:** "Thank God I'm finally dead," I whispered, laughing to myself.

**Bible:** *"Those who plant in tears will harvest with shouts of joy. They weep as they go to plant their seed, but they sing as they return with the harvest"* (Psalm 126:5-6 NLT).

3. **Mood:** An emotional response that the writer wants to create in the reader with the words and descriptions found in the story.

**Short Story:** "I began to sob as I watched my books float amongst the crowds of people. I knew every cover. I remembered penning every word and publishing every manuscript. Millions of words and tens of thousands of hours I offered to the Lord in my lifetime were now alive and active. They were like my children being carried on the hips of kings and queens, and they shined so brightly that my chest heaved with immense joy. Something lifted from my shoulders, and I felt like a balloon rising. I looked to my Lord."

**Bible:** *"O LORD, how long will you forget me? Forever? How long will you look the other way? How long must I struggle with anguish in my soul, with sorrow in my heart every day? How long will my enemy have the upper hand? Turn and answer me, O LORD my God! Restore the sparkle to my eyes, or I will die. Don't let my enemies gloat, saying, 'We have defeated him!' Don't let them rejoice at my downfall. But I trust in your unfailing love. I will rejoice because you have rescued me. I will sing to the LORD because he is good to me"* (Psalm 13 NLT).

4. **Motif:** A repeated element, image or idea in a story that has symbolic importance and contributes to the meaning of the work.

**Short Story:** The main character in the story reiterates many times that her life was average and that she did not accomplish anything grand or special. I wanted to exaggerate this motif, so when she saw what her faith accomplished, the taste of a desire fulfilled would be more meaningful and impactful.

**Bible:** The Bible is full of motifs. One of the most important being the coming of a Savior and Messiah, Jesus Christ, which is demonstrated all the way back to Genesis when Abraham was to sacrifice his son, but God gave him a ram for sacrifice instead (Genesis 22:13). To Moses and the Hebrew slaves who put the lamb's blood on their doorpost to ward off the Angel of Death (Exodus 12:13). Even Jesus Himself alludes to His sacrifice as our Savior by saying the Temple will be torn down and rebuilt in three days (John 2:19). Other motifs include Living Water, the Wilderness and the Promised Land, Blood and Wine, Bread and Body and Walking by Faith.

5. **Point of View:** The perspective from which a story is told, including first person, second person and third person.

**Short Story:** I wrote this story in first person because I wanted to make a statement of faith of my God-given promises through my own writing.

**Bible:** The Bible (Old Testament and New Testament) is written in all three points of view.

- First Person: *"In my former book, Theophilus, I wrote about all that Jesus began to do and to teach until the day he was taken up to heaven, after giving instructions through the Holy Spirit to the apostles he had chosen"* (Acts 1:1-2 NIV).

- Second Person: *"He will not let your foot slip—he who watches over you will not slumber; indeed, he who watches over Israel will neither slumber nor sleep. The LORD watches over you—the LORD is your shade at your right hand; the sun will not harm you by day, nor the moon by night. The LORD will keep you from all harm—he will watch over your life; the LORD will watch over your coming and going both now and forevermore"* (Psalms 121:3-8 NIV).

- Third Person: *"Instead, the men did their best to row back to land. But they could not, for the sea grew even wilder than before. Then they cried out to the LORD, 'Please, LORD, do not let us die for taking this man's life. Do not hold us accountable for killing an innocent man, for you, LORD, have done as you pleased.' Then they took Jonah and threw him overboard, and the raging sea grew calm"* (Jonah 1:13-15 NIV).

# CONCLUSION

I couldn't write about several basic literary devices—like alliteration (repetition of beginning sounds of words in a sentence) and assonance (the repetition of the internal sounds of words in a sentence)—because the Bible has been translated from its original three languages. However, they do exist in the Hebrew, Greek and Aramaic. I didn't want to do a language study for this book, and those devices are mainly to tantalize the readers' or listeners' ears. You will find them in abundance in my short stories, though. I enjoy searching for synonyms of words so the sounds in a sentence stay the same, but the meaning is still similar.

I thoroughly enjoyed writing this book. It challenged me to be more creative in my writing. In fact, I altered several of my short stories to add more literary devices. I believe the devices developed the stories and created more of an interesting read. I know that when we read the Bible with that mindset, we will gain more intrigue, insight and importance from our reading time. However, we must truly hear and meditate on the meaning behind the words. The Holy Spirit will guide us and make the truths written in God's Word our own, but we have to wrestle for them. It's like anything we do. The more we pour in, the more we receive, and knowing literary devices will help us receive more from God's Word, the Bible.

I am a firm believer in listening to sermons, reading Christian books and doing Bible studies, but we must also do our own meditation on God's Word. Receiving information is passive. Aggressively delving into learning is active. When I write about God's Word, I am meditating and actively thinking about what truth the Bible is conveying, so I can translate that truth to my readers. Writing has truly made me wiser in my faith. However, we don't have to write—though it is a great way of absorbing information—we can simply talk to God and listen to Him. He speaks sometimes audibly but mostly He speaks into our spirits—the part of us that is alive in Him where the Holy Spirit dwells. We can also talk to other Christians about our faith journey and what God is showing us. Conversations like these enlighten and encourage both people and/or groups of people.

Our world today has so many distractions, and we are so busy doing too many things and taking in too much information. We have to proactively set our TVs, phones and computers aside to connect with God. So many times, we pray out of desperation because of a situation we find ourselves in, but if we would have been praying proactively, we would have been more prepared. The Holy Spirit wants to tell us His secrets (Daniel 2:22). Also, when we speak in tongues, we can edify ourselves in advance (1 Corinthians 14:4). If you don't know what speaking in tongues is or how to do it, I suggest asking the Holy Spirit to help you and study resources based on speaking in tongues. Last of all, when we know not what to pray for, we can trust that the Holy Spirit will pray on our behalf (Romans 8:26).

I pray you enjoyed this unique book that mixes short stories, devotionals and literary devices together. That's one thing about God I know for certain: He likes to go against the flow and do something imaginatively new (Isaiah 43:19). If you feel your life is mundane or not making an impact, I suggest enthusiastically seeking God and His Word. He will have you do some scary, crazy, unbelievable and difficult things that seem impossible. But if you step out in faith into the void of the unknown, He will provide a steppingstone of His provision with each step.

> "And my God shall supply all your need according to His riches in glory by Christ Jesus" (Philippians 4:19 NKJV).

---

If you enjoyed this anthology of short stories, devotionals and lessons on literary devices, please leave a review on Amazon; so others may also gain understanding of literary devices and their purposes in the Bible.

www.ingramcontent.com/pod-product-compliance
Lightning Source LLC
LaVergne TN
LVHW010702110826
845149LV00014B/3193

*9781963190069*